JOHNNY HAVOC AND
THE SIREN IN RED

Pint-sized private eye Johnny Havoc joins
the circus to help a friend and meets the
mysterious Salome, she of the seven veils
and exquisite beauty. He soon uncovers
shady dealings beneath the big top, not to
mention mysterious doings at a nearby
army camp. His investigation pits him
against the US Army (including a barracks
full of beautiful—and naked—women
recruits). Havoc doesn't stop before he's
posed as a commander of the army and as a
spy for the Red Chinese. And always there,
luring him on like the Holy Grail, is
the indestructible, delectable red-haired
Salome . . .

JOHNNY HAVOC AND THE SIREN IN RED

John Jakes

CURLEY LARGE PRINT
HAMPTON, NEW HAMPSHIRE

Library of Congress Cataloging-in-Publication Data

Jakes, John, 1932–
    Johnny Havoc & the siren in red / John Jakes.
      p.   cm.
    ISBN 0–7927–1412–1
    ISBN 0–7927–1411–3 (pbk.)
    1. Large type books.   I. Title.
    II. Title: Johnny Havoc and the siren in red.
[PS3560.A37M35   1993]   92–37298
813'.54—dc20   CIP

Published by Curley Large Print, an imprint of Chivers North America, by arrangement with Sobel Weber Associates Inc., 1993.

U.S. Hardcover ISBN 0 7927 1412 1
U.S. Softcover   ISBN 0 7927 1411 3

Printed in Great Britain

INTRODUCTION

Like almost every other writer, I have often played a certain game. It's called 'Cast the Movie.'

After the book's out, you settle back and spin a pleasant daydream about a ringing telephone (nowadays a beeping fax machine), and an unexpected message saying this or that well-known producer or network out in the sunny Land of Oz wants—no, *lusts*—to put your work on screen, and will pay almost any price for the rights.

Whereupon you engage high-powered legal help to begin haggling on your behalf. And then, to the point of distraction—of others as well as yourself—you start to play the game.

I've played it many a time, with many a book. Never was the game over so fast as when I played it in connection with the four novels about my 5'1" private eye, Johnny Havoc.

Because I knew, from the first, exactly how Havoc should be brought to the screen (a weekly TV series, one hour per episode), and who should play him.

Unfortunately, the star I chose—(absolutely perfect; maybe I even concocted the first novel with him in mind)—never picked up one of the paperbacks and shouted to his agent, 'This part I gotta play.' Given the fairly limited distribution of original paperback mysteries back in the 1960s, I'm not exactly surprised that the Havoc novels failed to leap to his attention.

I began writing the Havoc books (a real miniseries, at four volumes only, if ever there was one) while I worked by daylight in the advertising business in Rochester, New York. I finished the quartet, with this book, while I was slaving away in the same game in Dayton, Ohio.

... Where the star I had in mind waltzed into town one summer, to do a turn in a stock season mounted at the downtown performance hall under the banner 'Kenley Players' (Kenley being an ex-Broadway hoofer who wisely decided there was more money in a short season of stock in Ohio than a year-long season of making the rounds in Manhattan).

I wasn't quite smart enough, or brassy enough, to carry the book down to the stage door and try to press it into the hands of the star, but I did *send* it to him, via the semi dependable postal service. I presume it was delivered to Memorial Hall in Dayton, where the star was appearing in some vehicle I've forgotten. But as to any response—the silence was, as they say, deafening.

So the star missed a big opportunity (in my opinion; his career was none too glorious right at that time.) And I missed a big opportunity to see the first Hollywood realization of one of my creations. Later, I had that opportunity, several times over. But I'd have liked it with Havoc, too.

Realistically, I was little short of an idiot to think it could happen. In the 1960s—even now, actually—producers do not exactly snatch up paperback originals for films. Three novels of *The Kent Family Chronicles* were spectacular exceptions to that statement. Yet the old class distinction between hard and soft covers prevails.

On the other hand, I think my casting, and the fast Keystone Kops action central to the Havoc stories, would have made for some great TV fare.

You may not recognize the name Fred Clark. Fred Clark was an exemplary, basset-faced character actor, long-jawed and bald, who could deliver a model slow burn whenever the director called for it. He typically played frustrated floorwalker types. I had him in mind for Havoc's nemesis, Detective Goodpasture. Fred Clark would have been a standout.

As for the star . . . surely I needn't tell you. Of course you guessed. Who *else* could play Havoc?

No one else. Only one short, knockabout, enormously talented gamin of an actor.

Only Mickey Rooney.

Well . . . maybe next time.

Meanwhile, my thanks to the Armchair Detective Library, Otto Penzler, and Ed

Strosser, for giving old Havoc this new lease on life. And between boards, yet.

Now if only those guys ran a film studio on the side . . .

John Jakes
Hilton Head Island.
South Carolina
23 April 1991

CHAPTER ONE

'*Well, sir,*' said I to myself at the very start of the mayhem, '*for an exponent of free enterprise you certainly have a delicate touch. You are, as the clowns in blue are wont to characterize you, a hustler.*'

This thought went sailing around in my dome as lightly as the warm and sunny Wednesday afternoon breeze that wafted down the streets of the amusement park, carrying with it the delighted shrieks and howls of terror of patrons on the Funnyland Blue Whiz Rollercoaster.

'*Yes, sir, you have a touch as light as a pick-pocket's on a bulging hip.*' And I deposited the very last of one dozen hardballs on the topmost point of the pyramid of hardballs which I had carefully stacked upon the wood counter of the pitch.

I stood back to admire my handiwork. Its execution had taken the better part of half an hour. One of the balls on the bottom of the pyramid gave a lurch.

'Hey, wait a minute, that's unfair, that's . . .'

The evil gods, like most everybody else on the side opposite to mine, were against me. The pretty pyramid shuddered and was no more. *Plonk-plop-kerbonk*. Balls dribbled this

1

way, that way, every which way.

'Wait a sec, hold on!' I cried, running hither and thither and scooping them up into the canvas apron which was part of the equipment supplied by my pal Irving Neely. Optically I hunted the missing balls. Two ... no, three, had dropped behind the counter and rolled down to rest against the base of one of the pedestals which bore pyramids of lead-filled plastic milk bottles. Where the fire was the last ball?

I espied it dribbling and fribbling its way across the park street, idly kicked by a teenager who sniggered at my expense, then dashed on to catch up with some of his pals. The sphere came to rest against the lower hem of the canvas of the pitch directly opposite the one I was staffing. The sign over the pitch platform proclaimed, *Salome Swanson's Hareem of the Seven Veils*.

So far, there had not been so much as a single veil displayed yonder. Platform and ticket stand stood empty. But that was typical, as most of the Funnyland pitches didn't open until mid-afternoon anyway. I had driven out early in my heap to look the grounds over, since today was my first day on duty in Irving Neely's stead.

I darted between a couple of strolling old fogies and watched my hardball surmount the resistance of the Seven Veils canvas and roll out of sight underneath.

Upon reaching the canvas, I bent down, I inserted my right hand beneath the edge of the tent, feeling around for the elusive spheroid. I wiggled my pinkies in air. Then I got hold of something.

I stuck my hand in a bit further. I seized the ball and straightened up, just in time to whack my head against a sudden obstruction upon my left.

A clutch of purple phrases sizzled the air. 'What the hell you doin', clown?'

The person against whom I had bonged had just been emerging from the tent entrance. He was a tall, thin, sandy-haired type. He wore slacks and a gaudy Ivy-stripe sports shirt. His blue eyes were about as pleasant as spoiled kumquats. He wore a crummy zircon ring on his little finger right, a showy chrome-plated wristwatch on his left wrist, and carried a hand microphone with the cord curled up around its base. As he stood about six foot three or perhaps more, my appearing before him in all of my five foot one magnificence made the scene resemble the confrontation between David and Goliath.

'I was hunting for my ball,' I said, displaying the object. 'My ball rolled over here.'

'Well, go back to the freak show where you belong, midget.' He massaged his gut. 'That head of yours must be made of cement. I ought to crown you for being so damn

3

careless.' He waved the mike. 'Go on, beat it.'

My dander was on the rise. 'I see no damn reason for you to get so testy.'

He squinted down at me. 'Haul it before I squash you and put you in a bug case, bud.'

Nothing is so calculated to arouse my anger as that type of remark about my size. 'I was going to apologize,' I said. 'But I guess I won't.'

About to climb up on the pitch platform, the sandy-haired type wheeled around. 'Just what the hell is biting you, little man?'

'Your damn rudeness, chum,' I said, trying to stretch to my full height, which isn't much.

Speculatively, the mean-faced type scratched his chin. He pointed at the canvas ball apron. 'You work around here? I mean, like you're new? You don't know the score about me, huh?'

'I work over there.' I thumbed toward the gaudy canvas sign over the ball pitch rig. The sign carried the nauseous legend, IRVING'S THRO-O-RAMA, SPILL 'EM AND WIN!!!

'Where's Neely?' he wanted to know.

'Gone to California, if it's any of your damn business. His boy is graduating college this week, which is obviously more than you'll ever accomplish. I'm standing in for him. My name's Havoc.' I did not feel compelled to add that being an amusement park pitchman

4

was not exactly my line of work. A temporary shortage of green presidential portraits, plus my pal Irving's inability to find anyone else to relieve him—he couldn't afford to close down because of inflation—had swayed me to accept his offer of a small percentage of the profits for operating the Thro-O-Rama through the weekend.

This set of circumstances had brought me out here to Funnyland Park this ostensibly cheerful Wednesday afternoon. But all at once, the whole shebang was far less than funny. The sandy-haired type was obviously in a wretched temper. My last remark about college had stoked his ire higher.

He reached over, snatched a couple of balls from the apron and whammed them, one, two, back across the street to the ball pitch.

His aim was deadly. The whizzing balls demolished two of the lead-bottle pyramids. Sandyhair glowered:

'As long as you're around this part of the park, midget, stay out of my way.'

I felt like sailing into him with both fists working. On the other hand, I'm a natural-born coward in addition to being a natural-born magnet for illegal green bills. I muttered something unprintably antisocial, and as he cursed and made a grab, I went rocketing off back across the street.

Shortly, I was safe behind the wood counter, the milk bottles re-stacked. I had commenced working on a fresh stack of balls. The sandy-haired item had climbed to the pitch platform. He plugged in his mike and blew into it a couple of times, darting me revengeful glances all the while. Several strollers strolled into the vicinity.

'Here you are, folks, right here, step right up,' cried I, flourishing three balls. 'Knock 'em over and win a high-quality prize from one of America's leading manufacturers, three balls for a quarter, only twenty-five cents, one quarter.'

A guy and his date paused, looked speculatively in my direction. I flashed my dentalware. 'That's right, sir, right over here, display the old eagle eye and powerful pitching arm. Just cough up ... er, surrender one quarter for three balls and you may win a...'

A veritable tidal wave of kootchie music, electronically amplified, eliminated all hope of further communication. The sandy-haired type had been out of sight below the pitch platform, and now I understood why. He had hooked up a phono that spilled the scratchy, deafening music all over the street.

The guy and his gal, my prospective customers, immediately did an about face as Sandyhair hopped up on the ticket booth. Darting malicious glances in my direction, he began to shout into the microphone.

'Awright, awright, awright, ladies and

6

genmun, step this way, right this way for one of the most scintillating an' sensual midway extravaganzers ever seen at Funnyland Park, the mystic secrets of the Oriental hareems unveiled by that delightful confection, that daughter of pleasure, here she is, to give you a little sample of the next performance which will begin in only ten minutes for just a dollar, that's all, folks, a dollar ... here she is, Salome!'

The tent flaps parted. Up onto the platform flounced a morsel to make my orbs distend with delight.

She was tiny. Around five feet, if I could judge. And being undersized in a world full of tall cookies, you have to have the right sort of eye.

Her eyes were bright blue and her figure very delicious in all its aspects, despite the fact that she did look somewhat hokey in a black Cleo-type theatrical wig and sequined bra and pants-with-several-veils hareem costume. The costume looked fresh out of somebody's silent picture costume trunk.

The morsel began to gyrate and rotate in rhythm with the music. Her pretty face was blank of all expression. Sandyhair continued his pitch and glared at her once in a while.

'Watch her go, folks, twisting, turning, and this is only a sample of ...'

A sizable crowd had collected. Most of them stared as though hypnotized at Salome

Swanson's highly active navel. The crowd was composed of young, not so young, and just plain old, and even included a Chinese in pince nez, a nifty two-hundred dollar suit and businessman's homburg. With true Oriental placidity, he contemplated the cookie's navel too.

More people were coming, attracted by the music and the pitch. They streamed in mostly from the right, from the center of the park. I watched them as they flowed around a big signboard posted in the center of the street a short way down. The sign announced in screaming red letters:

THIS PARK

OFF LIMITS

TO

ALL PERSONNEL

OF

FORT PERCY PARNELL

The Fort was some sort of government institution I'd read about in the papers. It was located in some woods way back of the park. Obviously the message had gotten across, for there was nary a trace of Army green to be seen in the mob.

'Step right up, now, let's have your money, the show's about to begin . . .'

While the morsel continued to grind in a disinterested way, Sandyhair leaned down from the ticket booth to make change and dispense pasteboard tokens. Though I

8

couldn't hear what he was saying, he was obviously still in a grumbly mood.

A porcine oldster handed up a mess of change. Somehow Sandyhair dropped it. Complaining, he climbed down from the booth and came around in front of the pitch. As he bent to retrieve the money, the crowd pressing forward thrust against the porcine oldster, whose paunch in turn contacted Sandyhair's head, whamming him against the wooden booth. Sandyhair straightened up, mouth twisting, cheeks scarlet.

'Watch who you're shoving, you Goddam blimp!' he howled, and threw a punch.

Delivered in a fit of temper, it wasn't much of a punch. The porcine oldster reeled back in feigned agony, however, clutching his corporation. Sandyhair stood with fist ready. The porcine oldster declaimed loudly that he was not going to stand for such treatment, and where the hell was the park management?

He went waddling off, followed by half the crowd.

Crowds are funny animals. And Sandyhair's display had killed all enthusiasm. The morsel had stopped grinding, and was standing with fists on hips, glaring at Sandyhair.

In moments, the rest of the crowd melted. Sandyhair was obviously thinking of something else besides me, so I hunched back inside the shadows of the ball pitch, chuckling in delight at his discomfiture. The morsel snatched off her black Cleo-wig and threw it on the platform and stamped on it, her yellow hair sparkling in the sunshine.

'Lou Cyrus,' she said, 'that was absolutely uncalled for! We might get sued!'

'I'll break the old gas bag's arm if he tries anything like that,' said Mr. Cyrus, but with some degree of hesitation. 'He pushed me.'

'I've had just about enough of your vile temper,' the blonde said. 'And don't pull the innocent bit on me, Lou Cyrus. I heard about that fight you had. How you beat up that perfectly innocent fellow Edson for no good reason. It just shows you what kind of bunch you run around with. Gang fights!'

'My God, Judy, cool down,' responded Cyrus. 'It wasn't me. It was Fogel, Kewpie's boy.'

'Fogel!' snorted Judy. 'Kewpie! Your friends! You're all a pack of hooligans!'

'Ah,' Cyrus snarled, 'that jerk Edson had it coming. I tell you, Judy, there's something phony about that Edson and his long, horsy jaw. Fogel should have creamed him, just like he did. Edson's probably a damn spy the Slotnick mob planted. You know how the Slotnick mob's been trying to cut in on Kewpie's concessions here at the park.'

'Concessions my foot!' was Judy-Salome's reply. 'It's an out-and-out strong arm operation and we both know it. I wish the management would get rid of Mr. Kewpie North, and that brute Fogel, and take you along with them, since you're all so palsy-walsy.'

'Listen, Judy,' Cyrus whined, suddenly contrite. 'We won't get any business standin' here all day hollering at each other.'

'We won't get any business at all the way you're assaulting the customers!'

And the argument continued on slightly lower vocal levels because people were beginning to drift through the area again. A couple of sailors with girls on their arms paused in front of the Thro-O-Rama and, reluctantly, I began flourishing balls again.

What was happening across the way was none of my apples, actually, except that little Miss Salome-Judy was a damned cute trick, and just my proportions. Still, business was business.

'How about it there, sailors?' I said brightly 'Only a quarter, three balls.'

'Oh,' cooed one of the girls, 'why don't you try, Ardmore? I'd love a stuffed doll.'

'Well uh, O.K.,' said Ardmore, who was underfed and wore glasses. He paid his money, swallowed hard, his Adam's apple bobbing as he muttered uncertainly, 'Give me some room, there.'

Ardmore began a fantastic whirling windup. I stood placidly to one side, arms folded, watching his arm go round and round

11

and round and...

The ball wasn't in his hand any more.

The ball was–

'Owwwww, oh Goddam it to hell who the ... *you?*'

The strangled cry from across the thoroughfare told me the worst.

Dimwitted Ardmore had launched the ball, all right, but accidentally, and backwards, during his flying windup. The ball had sailed through the air as if directed by some malignant powers bound to land me in the soup, and conked Lou Cyrus right on the noggin.

Ardmore's girl-friend began to plead desperately for the group to absent itself, and I had a thrilling view of Cyrus stalking toward me across the street, massaging his pate with one hand, holding the ball in the other. I noticed with some alarm that Miss Judy-Salome had vanished. Huffed off into the tent, no doubt.

Ardmore and his friends decided that duty called somewhere else, and faded rapidly from the scene. Not wishing to be trapped in the narrow confines of the milkbottle pitch, I hopped the counter and confronted Lou Cyrus in the street.

'I'm going to ram this ball right down your undersized throat,' he announced.

'I didn't throw it,' I shot back, growing intemperate again. 'But you're welcome to try.'

'Trouble, there, Lou buddy?' said a new, menace-fraught voice.

My cowardice index soared to new heights as I noticed for the first time the group of three plug-uglies who had been loafing along in our general direction for some moments. They wore cheap suits, the garment of the leading member of the group being a particularly horrid shade of green. This leading specimen had thin, plastered down hair and eyes the shape of cue balls.

'Hullo, Fogel,' said Cyrus. 'Hullo, Buster. Hullo, Rix. I can handle this.'

'Well, if you think so, sure,' said Fogel, surveying me with his unusually large orbs in which glowed not a whit of human kindness. 'We were just cruisin' around and it looked like you needed some help. That's what friends are for, ain't it, Lou baby?'

Fogel, Lou Cyrus had said. The morsel had mentioned Fogel, and something about gang beatings. All at once, I seemed totally alone in the midst of the few people drifting this way and that along the street.

Cyrus gave a scowl, hooked a thumb. 'This little punk showed up here at Neely's pitch today. He's been giving me a hard time. Says Neely is off in California some place. He beaned me with a ball, the craphead.'

'It was one of my customers who actually—' I began.

13

'I'd shut up, peewee,' said Fogel with chilling cordiality. His oversized orbs seemed to vibrate with menace. Fogel cracked his knuckles. 'Stranger around here, huh? Listen, Lou, I'm sure you can handle this, but have you thought of this possibility? He just might be another plant by those Slotnick bastards.'

Lou's expression brightened. 'Sure! Damn, why didn't I think of that?'

'I never heard of Slotnick,' I said. 'You're making a big mistake. I warn you—'

'Warn, shmarn,' said Fogel, darting several glances. 'Lou, what say we take him behind your pitch over there and check him out? Been a kind of quiet afternoon anyway. Kewpie'd want us to be careful about spies the Slotnicks might of sent. Won't hurt if we're wrong.'

Nobody but me it won't, I thought, but before I could voice that opinion, they closed around me, and they were such big lugs, anybody who'd paid any attention—and nobody did—could hardly have been aware that they were half carrying, half dragging me.

'Now just a damn minute!' I kept saying, but that cut no ice at all.

Before I knew it, they had me set up behind the Salome pitch, in a shadowy alley formed by the backs of two rows of tents, and I was doing my damnedest to get off a punch

14

or a protest, but the creep called Buster had my arms pinned behind my back, and the one called Rix had his paw over my map.

'The Slotnicks sent you, didn't they?' said Lou Cyrus.

'They certainly did not,' I said when Rix took his fingers away. 'I swear, if you jerks lay a hand on me—'

'Yeah?' said Fogel. 'What'll you do, peewee? Call your Scoutmaster?'

'Tell Slotnick,' said Cyrus, 'to keep his boys out of Funnyland, hear? Out of Kewpie North's park, hear?'

'I hear,' I said. 'But I never heard of Slot—'

Ker-bam

Fogel gut-punched me hard, doubling me over. That set off the skyrockets of outrage, all right. I banged Rix and Buster in the midsections with my elbows, heard them go 'Oof!' and curse. But by then, Fogel's low blow had bent me from the waist, so that my jaw was exposed.

Lou Cyrus stepped up. 'Tell the Slotnicks this is what we do to the clowns they send around to spy on us.' And up from the pavement came his bunched knuckles.

I sailed back into the arms of Rix and Buster, who rained blows on me from behind in return for my elbowing. From there on, although I landed a couple of telling punches, it was a downhill journey. Fogel's egg eyes

15

positively bulged with pleasure as he told his cohorts to hold me up for the last set-up, which was a hammy fist that felt like it tore half my skull away.

With some very courageous outcries about how I would take revenge, outcries which unfortunately went unheard because they came out sounding like, '*Grrz, frmz, zappo, brritz,*' I slid down to the concrete and went achingly to sleep.

CHAPTER TWO

A professional basketball group was playing the game with my skull.

Bounce, bounce, bounce. Bong, bong, bong.

The floodlights in the amphitheater were gruesomely bright. Banks of them. I tried to holler up at the light gallery for the guy to throw the switch on a few. Apparently he got the message. One by one, they all went out, except for a pair of bright blue floods.

Which were not floods at all but the concern-filled orbs of the little blonde dancer.

'How many veils have you got on now?' I muttered, still not quite coherent.

Then I saw she had none. They were draped over a costume trunk, in one corner of a wooden-walled dressing cubicle. On the

16

wall a pinup lamp shone cheerily. That indicated it must be dark outside. Salome-Judy was wearing a sweater and skirt and a pair of low shoes. She sopped something damp against my forehead.

'Cut it out. Smarts too much.'

'Now you be silent.' She dabbed away briskly. 'Merthiolate. It'll keep the germs from multiplying.'

While I garrumphed and let her finish, I slitted my eyes and peered about in case Lou Cyrus was still lurking. He wasn't. She completed her task and brought a cup of hot coffee from a hotplate in the corner. Then she gave me two tablets featuring a combination of ingredients. Presently the basketball group left the court in my head.

I eyed her short, lusciously-proportioned person. 'Your name is Swanson. Judy or Salome, which?'

'Judy. The Salome part is a come-on for the marks—the customers. What happened to you, anyway? And who are you? I remember seeing your face this afternoon, over in the booth where Irving usually works. Is Irving sick?'

'He will be when he finds out what I'm doing to his business.' I sat up on the couch. 'The name's Havoc. John Havoc. And don't tell me you don't know what happened, sister,' I added, rather testily. 'It was your barker who made it happen.'

17

Up flew her eyebrows. 'Lou Cyrus?'

'It wasn't Captain Hook. Lou and a few other pals of his.'

'Honestly, I didn't know. Lou and I had a fight earlier this afternoon. Maybe you saw it.'

'Just like a soap opera.'

'Yes, wasn't it? Well, afterwards, I was so mad, I just had to get away for a while. I got dressed and went for a long, long walk. When I came back, I found you lying in a heap out in back of my tent here.' Her eyes snapped. 'And that's not all I found.'

She picked up a tin cash box from her makeup table. The lid hung by one hinge.

'Somebody robbed your vault?' I said.

'It must have been Lou. Before we had our fight, he hit me for a loan. Even though he is ... was—' (she made the correction with a slight pink coloring in her cheeks) '—my boyfriend, our arrangement here at the pitch was business. I paid him a salary. But it wasn't enough, I guess. After he roughed you up, he must have come in here and jemmied the box. He took every cent.'

Angrily she slapped the busted tin lid shut. She flung the box in the corner with a terrific whang. 'It's the first time he ever did something like that. I don't know what's gotten into him lately.'

'Sounds like you might be through with him,' said I, hormonally hopeful.

18

'You can bet a roll of dime tickets for the Whip I am!' She flounced down on the couch's edge, touched my forehead with fingers that lit me up with several thousand volts of body electricity. She smiled. 'The cut has stopped bleeding. Otherwise, you're just bruised.'

'But I'll never recover from the trauma. Not until I score one back on Mr. Cyrus. With your permission. Or—' I added this to test her, '—without it.'

'Be my guest. My, you're kind of cute. And just about my height. You have no idea what a chore it is, craning your neck to look up at tall men.'

I edged closer. 'Yes I do.'

'How do you happen to be working for Irving?'

Briefly I told the tale, concluding: 'Now it's your turn to fill me in on Mr. Cyrus. Especially that group of animated punching machines he hangs around with.'

'They all work, if you can call it that, for Kewpie North.'

'North. Somebody mentioned the name. Who's he?'

'A crook,' she said emphatically. 'A small-time crook. He runs Stardust Heaven. Maybe you've seen it, over on the other side of the park?'

'Don't think so.'

'The big place with all the gingerbread.

Looks like an old-fashioned band shell, only bigger. Well, Kewpie has a short order restaurant there, and a bar, and a dance floor too. But that's only a front. Stardust Heaven is the center of operations for the nasty little rackets he runs all over Funnyland.'

At the word rackets my instinct for the nearness of green bills perked up. 'What sort of rackets might those be, pray tell?'

Judy Swanson shrugged. The motion did magnificent things to and for and with her bosoms beneath the close-clinging sweater. I tried to concentrate on other aspects of the surroundings, namely the ceiling, but it was difficult. She said. 'Kewpie and his plug-uglies lean on all the little concession operators for protection money. The only reason they've never picked on me is because Lou is their buddy and hangs out with them. Lou has also mentioned some illegal crap and poker games for high stakes in one of the Stardust Heaven back rooms. I've never cared to learn too much about the operation. But it's obvious that Kewpie is a racketeer and lines his pockets with dishonest dollars any way he can.'

I frowned. 'How come they let such an operator in Funnyland in the first place?'

'Oh, the park manager, Pop Toombs, has been trying to find some legal way to evict Kewpie for a year or so. But Kewpie has an airtight long-term lease, I gather. He can't be budged, short of some actual evidence that he's done something dishonest. And he has most of the concessionaires so frightened of his thugs, no one's willing to turn in the evidence. But I know this much. Business at the park has slacked off a lot in the last year. He's already given the place a bad name. For one thing, no more soldiers from Fort Percy Parnell are allowed here. Off limits.'

'Um, I saw the signs. Let's see. There was a Fogel, and a Rix, and a Buster. Kewpie's troopers?'

'Correct. The whole crew is ghastly. All except Edson, that is.'

'Edson. I couldn't ... ah ... help overhearing your argument with Cyrus, you know. And you were talking about Edson then.'

Judy fixed me with a slow, merry, yet somehow smoldering stare. 'You don't miss a trick, do you? I have the feeling you're a lot more foxy than you let on, Mr. J. Havoc.'

'Get me alone some time and you'll find out,' I leered. 'About this Edson—'

'Why do you want to know so much about Kewpie's operation?'

'Well, I owe them all a score, hon. I aim to settle. First I have to know the layout. Edson, if I remember, is suspected of being a secret agent planted by one of Kewpie's rivals. Some bunch called the Slotnick mob?'

Judy nodded. 'Yes. Edson is a very funny

person. He's tough. I mean tough-looking. But he's sort of ... well ... a gentleman. He looks like a thug but he doesn't act like one. He's been hanging around with Kewpie's crew about six months. And he has absolutely the longest, hardest-looking, most scarred-up jaw I've ever seen on a man. That pop-eyed monster Fogel picked a fight with Edson the other day. Beat him badly. Oh, this whole place is beginning to make me ill. I'm sorry I ever left Waldingham's One Hundred and One Combined Shows and settled down here.'

Then a pixy light lit up her blue eyes.

'At least, I was until you woke up.'

Ka-woosh, she banged down on the couch again, threw her arms around my neck and did things to my torso region by placing her assets against me. With her pink mouth too close for abstinence, she said, 'I guess you'll think I'm awfully forward, won't you?'

'I would if I could think,' I said inanely.

'It's not just because I'm on the rebound. Or want to make Lou mad. I wouldn't show him up with just *anybody*—'

'Uh, could we wait a second here?' I said, attempting to disentangle.

Judy pouted. 'What's wrong? Don't you like necking? And other things?'

'I'm cuckoo about necking and other things. However, I came out here to Funnyland because I was financially embarrassed. So I'm wondering if I could hit you with a proposition—'

'I knew you'd see it my way!' she cried, arms-a-flying again.

'No, no wait!' I cried, wresting free. 'A proposition about the cash box!'

The pout returned. But I persisted. At the moment, greed was stronger than libido.

'Judy, what if I volunteered to do a good deed and swipe your cash back from Lou Cyrus? Would you ... ah ... consider, shall we say, paying a collection fee? Something on the order of ... ah ... twenty per cent?'

Now the dolly leaped up. She stood for a moment or so with dainty little fists on hips, and blue electric storms flashing in her glance.

'Why, you're nothing but a ... a little crook! A chiseller! A cheap hustler who...'

'That's not so!'

'What?'

'My girl, I'm a defender of the free enterprise system.'

'You're a crook!' She thought another moment or so. 'All right. I'll cut you in for the twenty per cent, Johnny. And not just because I need the money back, either. It's nearly five hundred dollars by the way. I'm willing to make a deal so long as you promise to come back for ... well, you know. Necking and things.'

I leaped up. 'Natch. Wouldn't miss it.

23

Look, where do you think I might find Cyrus, this time of what I gather is early evening?'

After gnawing her lip, Judy said, 'I'd try Stardust Heaven first. I mean second. Come here.'

This time I did not hesitate.

She clamped her delicious lips upon mine and we engaged in several stimulating moments of kissing and other fol-de-rol. Then, with a little 'Hmmm' of pleasure and a gasp, she said, 'You even kiss like a crook. But I still like you.'

She opened a door in the plywood wall of the cubicle. She pointed through an empty stretch of tent, to where a faint wash of electric lights seeped under the canvas.

'You can use the back way if you can stand the sight of some of your own blood on the pavement.'

'I can and I will,' I said, breezing out. 'It'll fuel the fires of vengeance all the more. You be here for a while?'

'Yes. There can't be any show tonight with that rotten Lou on French Leave.'

'O.K., I'll be back as soon as I can.'

I blew her another buss and breezed out into the twilight.

Since I'd been in shirtsleeves when the fracas began, I figured I'd better get into my proper armor. I crossed the amusement park street, above which strings of electric bulbs

24

had come on. I collected my Brooks Brothers jacket and my porkpie from Irving's pitch, then rolled down the front canvas and tied it. I set off at a brisk pace through the bedazzling splendor of a big amusement park at dusk.

Carousels whirled. Music dinned. A rubber-balloon clown ten feet tall hugged his paunch and bobbled up and down in front of the House of Laffs. The crowds were picking up. As I bobbed along, I saw that peculiar Chinese again. The gent with the pince-nez, homburg and snappy business suit. He was meditatively munching a floss of pink cotton candy, all by himself.

The gingerbread pile of Stardust Heaven appeared ahead. Its cupolas and cornices twinkled with colored lights. A few couples were hoofing it somnambulistically around the open-air dance floor to the beat of some turgid R & R music. There were a few diners in the small restaurant, a clutch of beer-guzzlers in the bar.

I assaulted the female cashier in the restaurant. She sat behind a register counter piled high with gum, Kleenex packs and film assortments. I inquired briskly as to where I might locate Mr. Kewpie North.

'Kewpie? Maybe in his office,' the old doll mumbled through her spearmint. 'Through that door, end of the hall. What are you selling?' she added wearily, as though calls by

25

vendors were the bane of her existence.

'Uh, a swell line of souvenir pennants.' I tipped the porkpie and buzzed through the door indicated.

The hall was dim, long. At the far end, some shadowy person seemed to be tampering with the knob of a closed door. My heels clicked the linoleum. He whipped around.

I bunched up my fists. But the sudden display of dentalware as he hefted his bulging briefcase and rushed toward me allayed my fears somewhat.

'Mr North?' he said. 'Hi there! I'm Harley Nutzell, Peerless Film.'

'Sorry.' I stepped under a ceiling light. 'I'm not North and I don't have my Brownie with me. I'm looking for North, though.'

'Oh.' Harley Nutzell's smile faded. 'So am I. I was just checking his office. He's not in there.'

'Thanks, I'll wait.'

He took out a memo pad and flipped through it. I asked with some curiosity, 'Is there a lot of sales activity around this part of the world?'

'Oh yes, the South Shore is very brisk in sundries, very brisk.' He checked his watch. 'Hmm. Guess it's too late to make any other calls. Have to come back tomorrow. Incidentally, you didn't see any other fellows who looked like salesman at the bar, did you? You know, with sample cases?' He grinned.

'Kind of overspent my draw this week. I'd like to belt one before I go home.'

'Didn't notice anybody at the bar except some types in sport shirts.'

'Oh, too bad. I'll have to try the other spot.'

'Other spot?'

'Yes. You see, the bar here at Stardust Heaven is one of the two places in the area where you can usually find at least one member of the sundries selling fraternity. Nice to know when you're short of cash. We exchange loans. Well, don't forget me if you ever need some film assortments.' He handed me a card. 'Harley Nutzell. Junior.' And off he waltzed in a Dale Carnegie daze.

I shook my head and proceeded to the end of the hall. You could have heard a mouse scream in the silence. I eased the office door open. I edged through and stood a minute in front of the desk. On top of it, somebody had left a single green-shaded lamp burning. There were a few tattered invoices lying on the blotter, but nothing much else.

Mr. Kewpie North's office seemed to be located at the rear of Stardust Heaven. At least the dance music dinned in the far distance. A closed door led to some kind of alley visible through a dusty, fly-specked window. Outside it was full dark now.

I noticed another closed door on the right. Trying to figure an angle on how I might arrange a business session with Kewpie, should he return, I started rummaging in the desk. In a lower drawer I came across a mean, blue-metal cannon with a loaded clip.

Could I bluff 'em into thinking I had fetched back some extra shock troops?

I opened the wall door. It led into a sort of storeroom. I dragged a straight chair in there. I turned it around, propped the cannon carefully on top, then wedged the door shut and crossed the office to study the effect.

Pleasing, pleasing. It looked as if some unseen gunman had his cannon pointed out through the crack in the door standing slightly ajar. The muzzle was aimed straight at the desk.

I tapped one foot. Another.

I was wondering how long the wait would be. I wondered if my effect with the rod was too hokey. But I didn't wish to confront them absolutely cold. And if more than one came back ...

More than one was coming back.

My gut clutched up. Footsteps rattled in the hall. Then low voices. I listened hard. I thought I detected the tones of Lou Cyrus and pop-eyed Fogel. The footsteps came on at a leisurely pace. I backed against the wall next to the protruding gun muzzle, breathing hard, waiting ...

Where the car came from, I'll never know. But all of a sudden, its headlights washed across the dirty window, flicked away. Out in the alley there was a loud thump. A violent slam. A clash of gears. The whine of peeling rubber.

My immediate reaction was that some kid hot-rodding through the back byways of Funnyland had hit a pedestrian. Wait for the boys or give First Aid? Mope that I am, I scuttled for the rear door, eased it open. I took two steps into the alleyway...

And felt extremely un-funny extremely fast.

Twisted and ugly, a man lay not six feet from where I stood. He had not been run over. A bullet hole showed in the middle of his forehead.

Of the car there was no sign. I did a double-take when I noticed the stranger's peculiarly long, scar-ridged jaw.

'Edson?' I whispered to myself.

'What the hell...?' Lou Cyrus croaked behind me.

'It's the little peewee!' Fogel cried. 'Grab 'im!'

'Screw that noise!' I shouted, spinning around with my fists ready. 'You aren't going to stick me with—'

Cyrus brought the desk chair down on my head.

I reeled back against the doorframe, giddy-dizzy. Fogel crowded in to land a lump with his fist, checked at the last second:

'Lou. Lou, look! Lyin' there. Holy kimono! It's Edson!'

'Drag ... him ... inside,' Cyrus panted, between punches at my midriff. I got off one good, sizzling punch that rocked Sandyhair to the balls of his sneaks, and glassed his eyes a moment. But that was all. Fogel flipped open the lapels of his cheesey green suit and out came a cannon.

Fogel let out a shout and sailed the cannon through the air. Cyrus caught it just as I was sailing forward with both hands balled, trying to look taller and tougher than I felt.

'Right there!' Cyrus said. 'Right there, you little murdering bastard.'

'Murdering! Wait a minute, you've got the wrong slant on—'

'One side,' Fogel snorted, bumping me hard from behind. I pitched over on my map. Next thing I knew, Fogel had dragged Edson's corpse inside.

Fogel was just turning back toward our little tableau when the veins in his eyeballs began to pulsate. 'Lou ... Lou ... the next room. Watch it!' And with an hysterical yell, he launched himself forward like a lineman.

Unfortunately the cannon propped on the chair in the door slit did not offer a great deal of resistance. Fogel came up spitting and cursing and gnawing some splinters. He kicked open the door, rod in hand. He flipped the light switch on, off. Then he gave out with a snigger.

'Peewee had the cannon rigged. Of all the hokey stunts!'

Lou Cyrus stared at me with malicious eyes. 'We had Edson figured all wrong, Fogel.'

'Howzcome?'

'Would he get the chill from this slob of the Slotnicks if he was a Slotnick himself?'

'I guess not.' Fogel stared down at Edson's unpretty corpse. 'Poor sonofabitch.'

'Listen,' I said, sensing the trouble worsening by the split second, 'I am not a member of the Slotnicks crowd. That guy was dumped in the alley by a car that passed just before—'

'Lousy liar!' Cyrus howled, and whacked me across the jawbone with the cannon.

I ping-ponged off a couple of the walls. I had to brace myself in order to stand up. Cyrus righted the desk chair. He sat down. He said:

'Kewpie's away on a short trip, creep. But he's due back any time. I think we'll hang onto you until he gets here. I figure he'll want to take care of you personally. Kewpie won't care for you having bumped one of his own boys, even if we did have the boy figured as a ringer. Don't you think we ought to hold him, Fogel?'

'I sure do.'

'Don't you think Kewpie will want to fix

31

him personally?'

'If he doesn't,' said Fogel, his knuckles cracking like my bones soon might be, 'I will.'

CHAPTER THREE

With that unpleasant pronouncement ringing in my ears, I next heard Cyrus declaim, 'We better get the stiff stashed out of sight, Fogel. You also forgot to shut the door.'

So cueball-eyes had, in the excitement of discovering what he believed was an unseen gunman in the next room. 'Okay,' Fogel said, 'but let's throw peewee in the storeroom first so he don't try nothing.'

The uglies grabbed me by the elbows and marched me to the connecting door. Fogel snapped on the light, revealing a windowless chamber piled high with cartons of bar supplies, tissues and assorted sundries. Festoons of cobwebs hung from the ceiling corners.

'Pick out a nice soft bed, any bed at all,' Fogel chuckled, waving at the ' dusty floorboards. 'You may have quite a wait before Kewpie gets back. We want to be sure you're on hand to—'

'Damnation!' That was Cyrus, who had left. 'Fogel! Quick!'

Still with a tight grip on my person, Fogel turned around. Cyrus had dropped down behind the desk, was peering out in a posture of alarm. Fogel quickly darted back inside the storeroom.

From somewhere outside, a reedy voice piped, 'Oh, mercy to goodness.'

With a slight wriggle I managed to get a glom. A feeble-looking elderly person had stuck his head in through the half-open alley door, and was goggling behind his bifocals. The gent wore a gaudy uniform with a shoulder patch identifying him as a Funnyland attendant. The brown paper lunch sack he held in one hand was shaking like leaves in a storm.

The old party gave a last tremulous mumble, in which the word police was audible. Then he whizzed off into the darkness at a run.

'Thought nobody ever used the damn alley but us,' Cyrus whispered, rising.

Fogel was sweating. 'That old jerk must have been taking a shortcut to work. What are we gonna do?'

'Why don't you try throwing yourselves on the mercy of the courts?' I suggested.

Biff! Cyrus delivered one against my chops that sent me up against a stack of boxes. One bounced against my porkpie. I sat on the floor, dizzy, as Cyrus attempted to think out the ramifications of the situation.

'What do we have to worry about?' he decided finally. 'We didn't cool Edson. It's for damn sure Kewpie didn't. So all we got to do is pretend we discovered the body if they haul us in, and play it innocent all the way. We may be in a mess for a while, but our only real problem is him. The midget. I mean, since we know who really cooled Edson, we got to keep the blue boys as far away from this room as we can. Kewpie wouldn't like it if we muffed things so that the cops squared the rap with the midget, not Kewpie himself.'

Fogel said, 'But we can't move the body. And midget here might yap too loud.'

Cyrus snapped his fingers. 'The cellar!'

'Yeah, the cellar!' said Fogel ghoulishly, and the cellar it was.

They pulled me into the hall, dumped me down a long flight of wooden stairs, and the heavy door went *thud*, locked tight. I bumbled around in the darkness for a while, tripping over all sorts of packing cases and hitting my head against the runs from an old iron furnace.

If there was a light switch, I couldn't find it. I could hear nothing, see nothing. I opined that since no sound reached me, no sound I made would reach anybody upstairs or outside. Consequently my best bet, though a lousy one, was to wait and see what developed.

I settled down to try to snooze. But the

34

state of affairs was too tense for that. I climbed up on a pile of cartons to hunt for window openings. The pile collapsed. I collapsed with it, on my pratt.

And all, I thought wretchedly, because of a miserable yearning for twenty percent of the loot in Judy Swanson's cashbox.

Exactly how long I languished belowstairs I did not discover until my release. Actually it was all of that night and most of the daylight hours next day, Thursday. I was practically ready to bite my fingers, I was so hungry. I did catnap a little, but not much. Now and again there would be very faint taps overhead, the merest echoes of footsteps. Nothing else.

When the door at the top of the stairs finally did click again, my friend Fogel was back. Plus the toughie named Rix.

'Kewpie wants to see ya,' said Fogel, as they rushed down the stairs and manhandled my person back up again. Rix gave me a couple of kidney punches just for sport. As they razzle-dazzled me down the long hall, I got my first clear look at my watch in close to twenty-four hours. I blinked furiously in the light.

At the desk in the office sat a small, rubicund gent with fat gopher cheeks, highly tonicked black hair slicked straight back over his round skull, and a plastic-tipped cigar in his face. On the desk before him lay one of the morning rags from the city. Upside down,

I could make out a screamer headline which included the word *Murder*, and a two-column cut of Edson, long jaw and all.

Fogel and Rix manhandled me forward, shut the door and backed it up with their spinal columns. Rix unbuttoned his jacket suggestively so that I could not fail to see the cannon-butt hanging in a shoulder outfit.

'I'm North.'

'And I'm Tinker Bell, queen of the fairies,' I snarled. 'What the hell is this?'

'What'd you say his name was, Fogel?' Kewpie asked. 'Hammock? Hassock?'

'Havoc,' I said. 'J. Havoc. Innocent citizen. Listen, you cheap crook—'

Kewpie tittered nastily. 'Listen to the pot callin' the kettle black!' All at once he skyrocketed up from his swivel chair, rushed around and began to manipulate my shirt front, bouncing me up and down.

'Watch it, watch it!' I exclaimed. 'That's a Hathaway, I paid nine dollars for—'

'I thought the Slotnicks had better sense than to send a fink,' Kewpie interrupted.

'The Slotnicks didn't send me! I don't know the Slotnicks!'

'Crap on that.' He released me and exhaled a few puffs of cigar smoke into my eyes. 'You weaseled in here on orders from the Slotnicks, and you burned Edson because you figured out, don't ask me how, that my boy Fogel here had a fight with Edson the other

36

day. So you decided—or the Slotnicks decided—to shoot Edson, dump the body right on my doorstep and pin it on me and my lads. Well, little man, I ain't going to be pinned. Hear?'

'Hey, chief,' said Fogel. 'Let us try. We'll make the peewee squeal.'

'Nah, wait a second.' Kewpie's black eyes focused meanly upon me. 'Havoc, lemme lay it out. You might as well confess to shooting Edson now, when you got all your bones whole, as later, when you're lyin' on a stretcher like a Jell-O dessert. Because, little man, one way or another, I am gonna get that confession. And then I am gonna turn you over to the coppers, with my compliments, as the dastardly hired assassin of the Slotnicks. Kind of neat, huh?'

By this time I was really sore, and had temporarily forgotten that they all outweighed me a mile. I shoved out my jaw and cried, 'Peachy, Kewpie North. Just Peachy. Except you've got the wrong damn number. I didn't blast your man Edson.'

'The boys caught you.'

'The baloney they did! I swear, mister, if you don't release me, and quick—'

'I ain't releasing you until you confess!' Kewpie howled, damaging my shirt again.

'And I'm not confessing no matter how much you work the menace routine!' I shouted back.

Kewpie untwined his fingers from my shirt fabric, stood back. He shook his head. Then, at the corners of his nasty little mouth, a smile curved. And curved. Wider and wider, until I began to get a decided chill within my person. He shrugged.

'Suit yourself, little man. You won't cough up on your own, O.K., we'll get the confession another way. Rix? Fogel? Our guest here. He needs some calisthenics.'

With a horrendous crack of his knuckles, Fogel moved forward. 'Yeah, chief. Some physical education, huh? Only the kind that don't build you up...'

Whap! The blade of Fogel's left hand chopped me in the neck. I chewed some rug fibers.

'—it's the kind that tears you down. Bit—'

Rix used my head for a football.

'—by bit.'

So did Fogel.

By now I was crawling around on all fours like a drunken pooch. Feathered friends, wholly imaginary, tweeted inside my aching skull. I shoved myself up with my palms, drew back my right fist to punch Fogel, but had difficulty deciding which of his two ... no, three ... no, two, heads to belt.

Rix darted in under my guard and laughingly boffed me in the belly. I slid across the desk, cussing to myself like crazy, promising to square it all, someday. Fogel snatched me from behind. He bent my left arm up next to my spine and began to practice some criminal osteopathy on my bones.

'Ow, you bastards, ow, you rotten jerks, I'll get you for this...'

Kewpie stepped in front of me. 'You chilled Edson, right?'

'Wrong! Wrong, you lousy, oatmeal-faced—'

'Elevate the arm a few more inches, there, Fogel,' Kewpie instructed.

Fogel proceeded to elevate it so far, I nearly elevated clean out of my skull. I heard a door bang open. A sudden series of shouts and babbles from far off. Then a door shut. Fogel released me. I flopped on the rug. From that position, I observed that Lou Cyrus had rushed in.

'Kewpie, there's trouble out front. A real donny-brook.'

'You handle it,' snapped Kewpie. 'I can hear it, too. Who's doing all that screaming?'

'One of those crummy salesmen who calls on this place. Some guy named Hicks. No, Wicks. He wants to see you.'

'Tell him I'm busy. Doing calisthenics.'

'Yeah, but he's drunker than a lord. He's babbling a lot of nonsense about spies and Chinamen out to get him. And he's yelling about eighty-five grand.'

This last perked up Kewpie's attention.

39

'Did you say eighty-five grand?'

'That's right. Near as I can tell, this Wicks says there's eighty-five grand lying around waiting for somebody or other to pick it up, in return for ...' Cyrus halted lamely. 'I dunno what. Something. Something unknown. He didn't say anything about that. Buzz is working the bar. He was going to slug this Wicks and give him the heave-ho, but I thought maybe the talk about the dough was something you were in on. After all, eighty-five grand...'

'Eighty-five grand,' Kewpie repeated wistfully. Then, brisk: 'Nah, he must be just another drunk. Cool him down. I can hear him alla way back here, and I don't want any more attention from the coppers or the park management until I'm good and ready.'

Cyrus nodded, darted out. Kewpie wagged a finger at me. 'You ready to spill yet, little man?'

'I won't be ready until—'

I was interrupted by a furious knocking at the alley door.

'North? North! Are you in there?'

The handle was already turning.

'Haul him up!' Kewpie hissed to his bravos. 'Straighten his clothes, for Chrissake! It's that old gas-bag Toombs.'

Toombs? I thought blearily as they hoisted me against the wall and leaned me there in some semblance of genuine health. I tried to keep from falling over on my face as I recalled where I'd heard the name Toombs before. The alley door burst open.

Outside, it was growing dark already. This whitehaired daddy in a seersucker suit came stomping in. My head began to clear right away. At long last, here was some hope, some kindly soul from the outside world. Judy Swanson had mentioned that a Pop Toombs was manager of Funnyland.

Kewpie practically did the hundred yard dash getting back to his desk. He waved his cigar. Despite his smile, his dislike was evident. 'Oh, hiyah, Pop. How goes it?'

With a single glance that crossed me off as just another of Kewpie's pugs who had gotten bruised in a private brawl, Pop Toombs displayed his teeth and cackled, 'It goes just fine, North. It goes splendidly. And out you go, too, I am personally delighted to say.'

'Out?' Kewpie blinked rapidly 'Out? You wanna go for a walk or something?'

'For your information,' said Toombs, 'I just arrived back from my vacation about an hour ago. And I got the details of what happened in this den of ill repute last night. Namely, a dead man was discovered. One of your toughs, named Edson. I don't have any more details than that yet, but by heavens, that's enough for me to—'

'North? Kewpie North? This is the police again.'

41

Like that, pow, the hall door smacked open. The place was getting busier than a chiropodist's after the Memorial Day Parade. First came Lou Cyrus, who was firing hateful glances at his former girlfriend and trying to do a clog-step to bar the entrance of an officer of the law just behind her. I glimpsed a short, blonde-topped female form, and then a long-nosed, spaniel-eyed countenance, the sight of which brought a groan to my lips.

'Oh my God,' I said. 'Goodpasture.'

'What's going on here, North?' said Detective First Grade FitzHugh Goodpasture, marching into the room. He talked around the moist cigar which he always keeps in place in his eternally glum mouth. He spotted me and the mental pinball bumpers lit up. 'So it's true! There you are, Havoc, you little chiseler.'

'For a minute, Goodpasture, I thought I was glad to see you. Now, I dunno.'

Kewpie was ogling and goggling stupidly. It was clear from his expression that he had met Goodpasture before. Now Judy Swanson burst through the press at the doorway, rushed up to me.

'Johnny! Are you all right? I got so worried about you last night—'

'I know what's coming. You phoned the police.'

'Yes! I called the precinct, gave them your name, and told them you'd disappeared.'

FitzHugh chuckled morbidly. 'Naturally, John, that report came to my attention. As you probably know by now, I have issued standing orders that your name must always come to my attention. What are you up to this time, you little con artist?'

'Fitz!' I protested. 'Don't be unkind.'

'The only way I could be unkind is to let you remain at large indefinitely, to victimize the public,' he said.

Kewpie could hardly contain his irritation: 'Listen, cop-pe—uh, Detective. I thought you and me got all of our business taken care of last night.'

Pop Toombs leaped forward, addressed Goodpasture. 'I'm Toombs, the manager of Funnyland Park, Detective. Have you made the acquaintance of Mr. North?'

FitzHugh glowered. 'I certainly have. I headed up the detail which came out here last night after one of your attendants found a dead man in this office. Goodpasture is the name.' He flashed his buzzer. 'Mr. North was out of town, I gather, until shortly after my boys and I arrived. We had a long question and answer session about the corpse discovered on the premises. The corpse of a person named Edson.'

FitzHugh indicated the paper lying on the desk, added menacingly, 'I am not positive that I am quite finished with Mr. North, either. I won't be finished until we find out who committed the murder.'

Toombs practically dropped his dentures. 'Murder! Then the rumors are true? I just got back myself this morning, from Florida. Haven't even seen a newspaper.'

'All true,' said FitzHugh. 'Edson was shot in the head.'

'At last!' Toombs breathed. He clapped his hands. 'North, I've got you!'

'What the hell kind of crappy routine is this?' Kewpie chorused.

'Murder,' Toombs breathed. 'Murder—on these premises. At last, oh, at last I've got the lever I need to throw you and your crooked bunch out of Funnyland for good and all. The morals clause in your lease, remember?'

From Kewpie's pallor, he certainly did.

'Just a damn minute,' FitzHugh broke in. 'I'm interested in finding out what our undersized friend is doing here. For my dollars, Havoc is probably the shadiest character on the scene at the moment.'

'I second that!' Kewpie said. 'Believe me, coppe—uh, Detective, I'm going to be very cooperative. I'm going to be a very friendly witness.' He stepped closer, taking care to whisper loud enough for all to hear: 'My two, uh, associates here, Mr. Fogel and Mr. Rix, can offer evidence that the person who cooled Edson last night was—'

He gave me the fatal thumb.

'—him.'

44

Absorbing this, FitzHugh Goodpasture swung around slowly. Judy wailed, 'Oh, it can't be.'

But it certainly was, and I was wide awake and worried as hell.

Goodpasture's eyeballs had begun to spark with unholy light because—in the words of old Pop Toombs—at long, long last, it looked as though he had me.

'Well,' Goodpasture said cheerily. 'Well, well, well.'

CHAPTER FOUR

The moist cigar in Goodpasture's mouth began to work with an air of authority. My nemesis circled the desk, snapped on the lamp, then hauled down the shade.

'Out, out! Everybody out of here! I want to question this little bastard Havoc in private.'

Ever helpful, Kewpie said, 'But don't you wanna get my testimony, Detective?'

'If I want your testimony, I'll ask for it.' Goodpasture herded the crowd toward the hall exit, and they all began blabbering at once: Kewpie and his minions, Pop Toombs and Judy, whose outcries were the most plaintive of all. She dodged Goodpasture's outstretched paw, rushed back, and grasped the natural-drape shoulders of my Brooks

45

jacket, saying:

'Johnny, I ... oh, I hope I haven't gotten you into trouble by calling the police.'

'Oh, perish the thought,' I said.

'That detective glares at you in such a mean, menacing way.'

'Actually,' I said, 'he's suffering from stomach distress, fatigue, tension headache, not to mention—'

Spinning about on his worn-down Catspaws, Goodpasture croaked, 'I heard that, Havoc! All I can say is, keep cracking jokes. You'll find out how amusing they are when your appeal from a life sentence is finally turned down by the Supreme Court.'

He took Judy's elbow and propelled her after the gabbling mob in the corridor. Judy kept trying to tell me with tender glances all about her fears and regrets for me. Then Goodpasture slammed the door, obscuring the sight of Pop Toombs cackling and capering in front of Kewpie North, while the latter bunched his fists and glared at the old party who was about to break his lease. I also noticed in that instant before the door shut that Goodpasture had at least one other man with him, a plainclothes item who stood against the wall, surveying the mob scene from under a fedora two sizes too large.

Goodpasture's soles squeaked as he returned to the desk. 'Care to sit down, John?'

'Listen, to hell with the amenities, Fitz. I—'

'Detective Goodpasture, if you please.' He lowered himself into the swivel and owled me a moment. 'This time, I'm afraid, you have let your anti-social tendencies—your delight in denting, bending and actually breaking the law—go much too far.'

'Goodpasture, do you honestly believe that bonehead North? Why, you ought to know I never travel with the plug-ugly packs. I never even carry a gun. So how come you figure I'm mixed up in an obvious gangland chill?'

His gloomy orbs meditated upon my person. 'It goes deeper than that, this time.'

'What? Don't be so damn cryptic.'

'It goes much, much deeper, my lad. This time, you have overstepped the line from the other side of which there is practically no return. Don't you understand, you little shyster?' He whapped the blotter in an excess of temper which, for the first time, made me see that something unusual was up. 'This is a government case.'

'A government ... ?' That rocked me. 'Goodpasture, since when are you a Civil Service type?'

'Oh, for heaven's sake quit the wisecracks,' he sighed, rubbing the bridge of his nose. His eyes grew more spaniel-like each moment. 'I have been given some—no, too damn much—extra responsibility in this case, to

47

keep their connection quiet. They want their connection very quiet, Havoc. Get me?'

'No, I don't get you. Whose connection? The phone company's?'

'My God you're dense!' With furtive looks to either side, he leaned forward across the desk. He raised his hands, pressed the palms together, then wiggled them apart and brought them down, tracing some mysterious shape in the air. I shrugged, sat down on the desk corner.

'You want to play games, Fitz, okay. Animal, vegetable, or mineral?'

Once more he repeated the pantomime. 'Don't you recognize the capitol dome when you see it?'

'The capitol? You mean they is ... is Washington?'

'Of course I mean Washington.'

Portents of incarceration loomed. 'Fitz, hear me good. I admit I have flummoxed you a few times in the past. I admit I slice the corners sometimes, to make a penny. I suppose I've done some things I shouldn't to you and your men. But have you ever, for one single moment, known me to be mixed up in anything ... well, unpatriotic?'

'Never,' he said.

I started to relax.

'Until now.'

'Fitz! I didn't have a thing to do with shooting that guy Edson, if that's what you

48

mean.'

'That is precisely what I mean, Havoc. I'm not saying you did have anything to do with the killing. We'll find out if you did. Now I probably should keep quiet about it, as I am not the boss of the whole thing. On the other hand, you have a tendency to laugh off any accusation made against you by just an old, ordinary police officer like me. That gets us nowhere, ever. So perhaps I can convince you how serious this is, and make you talk sense for a change, by telling you that the dead man Edson was not a criminal. He was a plant.' Goodpasture paused. 'He was an operative of a U.S. counterspy apparatus.'

I felt as if I had swallowed a quart of rubber cement. 'Counterspy? Apparatus?'

'Stop gargling. You heard me.'

'Come on, Fitz. A counterspy working in an amusement park?'

'Titter all you want, Havoc. That doesn't alter the fact that Edson was operating under orders to recover documents which could mean a great deal of money if they fell into the hands of certain parties, not to mention a small disaster for this country if they fell into other hands which—'

The way he went rigid in his chair, I thought his cholesterol level had hit the top and he was due for a coronary any second. The moist cigar began working back and forth in his jaw at frantic speed. He bounded out from behind the desk, bowled me aside, and before you could say un-American activities, whipped open the hall door.

'Aha! I thought I heard somebody breathing!'

Doubled over at the waist, Pop-eyes Fogel regarded Goodpasture with discomfiture. 'I ... uh, officer, I lost my ... uh ... keychain around here. I was just looking for—'

'Get the hell away from that keyhole or I'll violate more civil liberties than you ever dreamed you had!' Goodpasture got hold of the collar of Fogel's green suit and gave it a yank. He hurled the hood against the wall, shouted, 'Hammerstein, what the hell are you doing down there, practicing Yoga?'

The hapless plainclothesman recovered from his snooze-like upright posture against the wall as Goodpasture finished, 'I told you to keep this hall clear and I meant it! Now take this ... gentleman ... back to the bar and make sure he stays there.'

Plainsclothesman Hammerstein collected Fogel and marched him away. Goodpasture slammed the door again.

'This is getting too complicated,' he muttered to himself. 'There's no telling whether those crooks are just crooks or...'

He stopped, darted a glance at me, clammed up. He paced a while.

'From past experience, John, I have the feeling that I will get absolutely nowhere with

50

you. Nothing but cutie remarks and yak, yak, yak. Well, I think by now you have gathered you have parties other than myself to deal with. Perhaps right now is the time to see what they want to do about this. I'm going to phone Washington to check up. But not,' he added, ankling for the doorway again, 'where you can hear.'

He opened the door. 'Hammerstein! Get you lead tail up here!'

The determined and somewhat overweight plainclothesman hoofed it to the office. Goodpasture pointed to me. 'Do not, I repeat, do not let this little chiseler out of your sight, or out of this room. I am going to make a phone call in privacy from that pay phone outside.'

'Sure, sir,' said Hammerstein.

FitzHugh opened the alley door and vanished into the mellowing dusk, where the amusement park lights were already gleaming, and carousel music added a false note of hysterical gaiety to what was rapidly becoming a mess.

I walked up and down, up and down. Hammerstein reached under his coat.

I froze.

'Care for a chew?' he said, extracting a packet of Wrigley's.

'No thanks, flatfoot,' I snarled.

'Well,' he growled back, 'if you want to be that way, O.K.'

51

My fate was an imponderable. The government involved? Mother! How? Why?

I couldn't answer. Step down, next contestant.

I had visions of myself in Leavenworth, or wherever they send undesirables. Always before, I'd been mixed up with nice, clean, murderous American gangsters who might plug you but who would always decorate your coffin with the Stars and Stripes. I wondered whether Goodpasture had lost a cog.

Surely there could be nothing so colorful and unlikely as a spy apparatus at the likes of Funnyland. Why, the whole notion was absolutely cuckoo. In a million years, no sane person would suggest that...

My spinal column went into deepfreeze.

Havoc, I said to myself, somebody has suggested.

'You sick?' said Plainclothesman Hammerstein. 'I have some Gelusils in my pocket.'

'Thanks, fla-uh, officer. I'll be O.K. Just let me sit down.'

He did, and I did, in the swivel behind the desk. Phrases kept coming back to mind. I'd heard them during my recent interview with Kewpie, when Lou Cyrus had come blustering in to howl that some guy at the bar ... Hicks? Icks? No, I had it, Wicks ... was yammering about spies. And about Chinamen, too.

Chinamen?

Hadn't I seen ... ?

Sure, twice. The peculiar type in the homburg and pince nez.

Oh, Havoc, this is turning into a Dali canvas brought to life.

Or was it?

What had Cyrus said? I couldn't remember it exactly, but I could swear the words something unknown were involved, and I never, ever forget figures.

I remembered the figure of eighty-five thousand clams.

Wow, It was like being offered the delights of eighty-five thousand harem lovelies.

I eyed Hammerstein.

I eyed the office.

I eyed my own situation mentally.

Do you suppose there really was that sort of loot floating around?

'Have a care, J. Havoc,' I cautioned myself. 'Remember FitzHugh is phoning the Capitol. When you get mixed up with the federals, you are in the big leagues.'

Still in all, the little green insect of greed was munching away at my innards, and in a rush I decided that my situation could hardly be worse. After all, what would I get from Goodpasture except lumps, a cell, and a fast ticket to some federal dungeon if they suspected me of cooling agent Edson?

On the outside, I might have a prayer of

discovering who had really fried the agent. What tipped the scale of decision was the fact that I represented a poverty pocket all by myself, and if I could snatch a percent of somebody's loose, eighty-five thousand clams along the route, it would be worth it.

I hoped.

All at once, I began to breathe a little faster. I tried to roll my eyes as though I were ill.

Hammerstein stopped munching his gum and swivelled his head.

'Say, what's wrong with you?'

I clutched the front of my jacket. 'There seems to be ... I feel ... oh. Oh. Oh.'

With a spasmodic expression upon my puss, I kicked against the desk and braced for the shock as the swivel chair went over backwards.

My dome collided with the baseboard. I lay with my legs up over the chair. The desk wastebasket, large, metal, was tilted on its side near my hand. Plainclothesman Hammerstein hotfooted clumsily around the desk while I gave another feeble pip.

'My pills, my pills! Oh, mercy! Inside ... coat pocket ...'

'I'll get them, I'll get them!'

Hammerstein knelt down. I attempted to be as gentle as possible in snatching the wastebasket from behind his back with my left hand and smashing it down on top of his head.

'Hey! Hey, for God's sakes what is this?' he cried, his voice now having a sepulchral tin echo. He managed to stagger to his feet. I did the same, grasping him by the shoulders and exclaiming, 'Look out, he's right behind you, detective!'

I thrust him hard and cut for the door.

The last I heard was a series of curses and the metallic thwonnnng as his whole person, including his head wedged inside the basket, struck the wall. I rocketed out the door and down the hall as quick as my sawed-off legs would carry me.

At the hall's end I slowed down. I tried to sidle casually through the short order restaurant. Unfortunately, Rix was having a java at the counter. He did a take and spilled the juice all over his lap as he leaped up.

Like a shot I zoomed into the cocktail bar. There were only two patrons. One was an old dame with henna hair. The other was (I hoped) the walking mint—a slightly inebriated type with a pencil mustache and, beside him on another high stool, a distinctive black leather attaché case whose silver initials gleamed in the muted light—H.T.W. H. T. Wicks, no doubt.

Up I rushed. I clutched his arm. 'Wicks? Hurry! Let's get out of here!'

'Wh ... ?' He threatened to fall off the stool. 'Whatzgoin on?'

'Wicks!' I hissed. 'Federal agent, Federal agent. Hurry! This way!'

'Federal?' he repeated foggily. I snatched the attaché case and that decided him. He followed.

Over my shoulder, I saw Rix scrambling through the short order restaurant. He yelled something to someone, but I was busy watching the expression on Wicks' face. The salesman's puss was changing as he blundered along after me. I was convinced somehow that what had put the pie-eyed look of bliss on his face were the words federal agent.

I hauled on his elbow, pulled him around a bend at the end of the bar, down another short corridor. It was dark, and just three lights glowed: one for Gentlemen, one for Ladies, one from the plexiglass front of a butt vending machine.

'Keep going, Wicks,' I panted, giving him a shove to propel him toward the door at the hall's end. I spun, saw Rix and the barkeep charging. 'Have a smoke!' I exclaimed, and tipped over the cigarette machine.

'Oh, ow, my God, oh hell, oh dammit, hit me right in the ... wow!' howled Rix as the Select lever struck his person.

Rix, barkeep and vending unit made a heap in the center of the hall. The barkeep flailed frantically to extricate himself, grasped the coin return lever by accident, and brought dozens of coins tinkling down into Rix's

56

open, cursing mouth. By then, Wicks and I were out that door into the dark.

We stopped. We were in the alleyway which ran behind Kewpie's office. Out of a patch of shadow across the way, a bigger shadow-lump disengaged. It lurched forward.

I caught my breath. Whoever it was, was nothing but a big, tall, featureless and sinister blob of black. Around me I scented the tang of cloves, as though the man had been munching them. Big gnarled hands reached out.

'Just a second, buddy—'

Those hands caught my windpipe. Then he released one hand while I thought crazily, A cop? The free hand smashed me in the middle belt region. Cops didn't punch that way.

I gave him the elbow, heard him laugh off the mere tickle at his midsection. 'Wicks!' I panted. 'Wicks, hit him! Bop him! Give him the attaché case in the skull!'

Dancing around from foot to foot, Wicks thought he'd better help the federal agent. Clove-breath jerked his head around as Wicks raised the case. I lifted my knee and knocked the wind out of the mysterious attacker. Then I gave him one short, vicious punch to the jaw.

It nearly broke my arm, but it disconnected his fingers from my neck, and it was enough. We were free. The Clove Monster reeled and cursed as he stumbled away from us.

57

'Follow me, Wicks!' I cried, tottering to the left. By then, other shouts split the darkness—Hammerstein's, Goodpasture's. Both of them boiled out of the recently vacated office of Mr. Kewpie North. A third officer in uniform followed.

'There they go!' Goodpasture shrieked. We did, and the hot pursuit was on.

CHAPTER FIVE

'What are we going to do?' Wicks caterwauled.

'Run!'

'Listen, who are—?'

'As a federal agent, I'm under orders not to reveal ... oh, stop jawing. Move!'

I gave him a shove in the shoulder blades which propelled him left along the alley. I shot around him, my eyeballs rotating fiercely in all directions in search of possible avenues of escape. I heard the slap of Wicks' loafers behind me. Further back, there was an assortment of yells, curses, and howls of outrage from Goodpasture, Plainclothesman Hammerstein and the uniformed officer.

The wall of Stardust Heaven ended abruptly. It was replaced by a gingerbread railing separating us from the open air dance floor.

'Follow me!' I yelled to Wicks, legging it over the railing.

In the flicker of light from one of those spinning glass balls every dance floor seems to have, I caught a blurred glimpse of his map. Wicks was sweating but sober. He seemed in good enough condition, and scared enough by the pursuit to keep up. I only hoped it would last.

'You people in there dancing stop those men!' Goodpasture shouted. 'They're wanted on suspicion of—'

'One side, folks, one side, please,' cried I, hot-footing it onto the dance floor.

Business had picked up at Stardust Heaven. There were about fifty or sixty souls paired off on the murky floor, ranging from a few old fogies who looked as though their idea of a snappy step was a waltz clog, to a bunch of teen boys and girls in tight pants and turtlenecks. Wicks and I barged through the fringe of the mob.

'Pardon me, this is an emergency, please let us through.'

We headed toward the dance floor's opposite side. Behind, Goodpasture and his aides were hauling it over the rail.

'There they go!' Hammerstein hollered.

Several couples lamped us, then the chasing bulls. Suddenly attention was diverted to the leader of the listless five-man combo on the bandstand. His satin lapels

59

shining in the spotlight, this worthy clutched the microphone to his jaws and deafened the air:

'Awright, awright, ladies and gennmen, time for the first dance contest of the evening, gran' prize one week's free pass to Stardust Heaven. Here we go, it's a rhumba! Olé!'

All at once the combo erupted into a pandemonium of bongo drums, maracas, ratchet sticks and other Latin appurtenances. Suddenly Wicks and I found ourselves trapped in the midst of a dozen shaking, writhing bodies.

'Pardon me,' I said, attempting to thrust by the gyrating hips of a teenage female whose pony tail was jiggling almost as fast as her sacroiliac. Bam, she bumped me. I said, 'Look, girlie, would you mind getting your—'

Bam, I got it again. This time it came from a fat, white-haired old bird with a Kiwanis button in his lapel. He was snapping his fingers in the air and wiggling for all he was worth.

Bam, Wicks got it and stumbled into me. Desperately I seized the shoulders of the teenage dolly from behind, and attempted to lift her to one side. Her eyes were glazed. Despite my hold on her shoulders, she kept her hips working:

'Go, Herman, go, go!'

Yips, yells, cries, gurgles, growls and other indescribable sounds issued from the dancers,

60

who seemed to have been thrust into a state of hysteria by the thumping, knocking tempo of the rhumba. Wicks and I were caught square in the middle of the mob. Goodpasture, Hammerstein and the item in uniform were weaving and dodging through the edge of the group now.

Carlos Kiwanis-button had pivoted by this time. His wife's posterior was now giving me the bam treatment. Well, there was nothing for it. I gave the begirdled expanse a pinch.

The harridan jumped and spun around, yelping, 'Molester, molester!'

'I saw everything!' I shouted. I pointed at the nearest teenager. 'He did it.'

'Did you put your hands on my wife?' Carlos Kiwanis-button trumpeted.

Whilst the teenage girl continued to rhumba with her partner absent, the teenage youth flicked the oldster's lapels with the back of his fingernails.

'You lookin' for a little action, pops?' he inquired threateningly.

'Everybody off the floor!' I exclaimed. 'It's a teenage rumble!'

This last phrase penetrated the din. Several women let out shrieks. 'A rumble, a rumble!' A sailor fainted. Goodpasture was almost upon me. I darted in between Carlos Kiwanis-button and the teenager, snatched the old lady by her begirdled waist and started propelling her backwards.

'My, you're a swell dancer,' I said. 'But someone's cutting in. She's all yours.' And, giving her a swift spin, I pushed her straight at Goodpasture.

At the moment of impact, he was trying to dodge. He was waving his hands, which unfortunately collided with her person around the bust region. The dame let out a foghorn bellow:

'Oh, oh, you filthy sex fiend, you won't violate my body ...' And she gave him a terrific belt in the puss just before the excitement got too much and she fainted.

Hammerstein and the uniformed officer attempted to relieve Goodpasture of the burden which had sagged into his arms. Meantime, I snatched at Wicks' elbow and angled my head at the gaps which had now developed in the crowd. People were yelling at each other, women were shrieking about wanting to get out of range of the gang fight, and the orchestra leader was vainly calling for order in the mike.

Darting past a few more bodies, I reached the bandstand.

'Police officer! I'll take over.'

Before satin-lapels could recover, I yelled two sentences over the amplifier system:

'Everybody stand still! This is a police vice squad raid!'

The alarms grew worse:

'Vice squad, vice squad!'

62

'No, it's a trick, it's a gang rumble!'

'Let me out of here...'

The rhumba contest ended in mass pandemonium, in which people fled Stardust Heaven, over the rails and even up the rainspouts, with an athletic ability that would have done the Olympics proud. Several fist fights had erupted. Poor Wicks was looking sleepy and more frightened than ever as I darted back to him, jerked my head and went scuttling for the pavilion's opposite side. What choice did the poor wretch have but to follow?

'That little man is impersonating an officer!' came Goodpasture's stentorian bellow. 'I demand that somebody stop—lady, if you kick me again right there, I'll arrest you for ... ohboyohboy!'

A hop, a skip, and I was over the rail dragging Wicks after me.

'Cripes,' I muttered, glancing in all directions, 'we haven't lost him yet.'

And so we had not. The three law minions, clothing askew, dispositions destroyed, charged ahead. Suddenly, just across the amusement park street, I noticed brightly shining double doors. Above them, a neon sign blinked on and off:

Uncle Clayton's Pancake Paradise

We had to stick to crowds until we got Goodpasture so tangled he'd never get free. The flock of hungry diners partaking of Uncle

63

Clayton's homemade batter looked to be the closest available crowd.

Wicks and I were just a few steps ahead of the growling, snarling, cursing trio of blue-boys when we batted through the doors into Uncle Clayton's fluorescent-lit joint. Aromas of warm, cooking batter and maple syrup made me dizzy.

The upholstered hostess stepped up.

'How many, sir?'

'Table for five. But here come the other three. Maybe you'd better ask them.'

And I gave her the heave-ho, propelling her directly into Goodpasture as he boiled in the door.

She shrieked. Goodpasture digested a mouthful of menus. I dragged Wicks down an aisle between tables of astonished eaters.

'What is it, Leland?' some dame cried. 'A labor demonstration?'

The aisle led to double doors similar to those by which we had entered. In between, however, were a number of obstacles, including a white-jacketed waiter carrying a heavy metal tray on his shoulder. The tray was laden with several platters full of pancakes, bowls of blueberries and strawberries, and a couple of containers of syrup.

'Keep your seats, folks,' I blathered as Wicks and I bumbled along. 'Food and drug inspectors, no cause for alarm. Just making sure the premises are up to snuff. Waiter, get out of the way. Waiter ... look out!'

The waiter was coming with the speed of a transcontinental jet, and muttering waiter-fashion out of the corner of his mouth: 'Coming through, hot, watch it, coming through.'

Behind, Goodpasture and the others were untangling themselves from the shrieking hostess. The tray of pancakes loomed. I backtracked furiously. Wicks had too great a momentum built up.

'Wicks!' I exclaimed. 'Put on the brakes or there's going to be—'

There was.

'Oh, God damn it!' bellowed the waiter as I caromed into the group. Up went the tray.

Down came dozens of pancakes, flying in fantastic arcs.

Splat. A gent got one across his forehead like an eyepatch.

Splat. A cookie got one down the back of her summer dress.

A syrup tankard cracked on the floor. We were suddenly awash in maple goodies. The waiter slipped. He sat down in the stuff, unloosing a flood of profanity, just in time for a flying bowl of blueberries to decorate his noggin.

Goodpasture's hands closed on my arm. 'Got you!'

Outraged diners began to leap up, ball their

65

napkins, shout for the management and their money back. Hammerstein fastened hold of poor Wicks, who was panting and near to tears by now.

'Aha!' Goodpasture crowed, shaking me violently. 'Aha! Inciting a riot! Damaging property! Oh, by heaven, Havoc, this time ... what are you doing?'

What I was doing was pouring syrup over his cuffs.

I had seized the syrup dispenser from an adjoining table, which may have been a nutty thing to do, but was also so unlikely and sticky that Goodpasture, whose cheeks were by now puffed-out and crimson, immediately reacted the way I expected he would react—without thinking, he jerked his hands back and tried to wipe them on his lapels.

The waiter had gotten up. He was lunging at me, fist cocked. I ducked. He bopped Hammerstein in the forehead.

That gave me the chance to haul Wicks loose. I shoved him around me down the aisle, just as the third of the law team saw his duty and came slogging on, through syrup and pancakes, trying to unlimber his holstered cannon.

By now I was so desperate, I didn't care what happened. Several diners tried to rush past me, as if they feared for their lives. One old broad had a fur cape around her shoulders, which I whipped off in a trice. The uniformed officer ducked in toward me, snarling. I wrapped the fur round and round his skull as the broad caterwauled:

'Eustace, oh my God, Eustace, my rabbit, get my rabbit back!'

'I'll fix you, you . . .' Hammerstein panted, forging on.

I let him have a bowl of strawberries. 'Here, catch.'

He had no choice but to try to get hold of the object flying through the air toward his skull. Unfortunately, he was butter-fingered. Or maybe syrup-fingered.

He touched the flying bowl just enough to deflect its course, at the moment Goodpasture ventured into the breach.

I tell you, a Detective First Grade with his pate decorated with strawberries is a sight not often seen.

When I tried to run, I discovered that my soles adhered to the tile by virtue of the flood of maple syrup. People were pushing, shoving, chorusing that the Red Chinese were rioting in the streets and other such nonsense. I spotted an opening, leaped up on an empty chair and off the other side. Wicks had managed to gain the exit already.

But Goodpasture, all a-drip and running with strawberry seeds in his eyelashes, was after me. So was Hammerstein. The uniformed type was still swaddled in the broad's rabbit, rolling around on the floor and getting plastered with more and more syrup.

I threw a chair into Goodpasture's way. Another.

He let out a curse and spilled over backwards. Hammerstein kept coming. Wicks and I dodged outside.

'He'll get us,' Wicks panted. 'He'll get us sure ...'

I espied an object sticking up from the grass plot outside the Pancake Paradise. I unearthed the stake with a few wrenches. Just as Hammerstein burst into the open, I hauled off and lammed him as hard as I could.

He stopped in his tracks. He goggled. Then his legs rubberized and he sat down and went to sleep, his chest decorated with the wooden sign which I had used for a conker.

The sign read:

OFF LIMITS TO PERSONNEL OF FORT PARNELL. This sign is U.S. Government Property.

So would I be, a ward of the Federal country club system, iron bars and all, when they caught me for this escapade.

Oh, hell. Hanged for a sheep and all that. I caught my breath and glanced at salesman H. T. Wicks. He was shivering something awful. Scared to death. But when I looked at him, I also saw eighty-five thousand beautiful dollars glimmering.

'O.K.,' I panted. 'Now we can run for it, and get away.'

We did.

CHAPTER SIX

We left the premises at a walk approximating a run.

Wicks kept muttering to himself. 'Horrible mess. Godawful, just Godawful. Federal agents taking the law into their own hands. Got to play along. Only safe way. She sold me out.' He chewed at the corner of his pencil mustache as though in extreme emotional distress. He still had that black attaché case in one fist.

'Where . . . where the devil are we going?' he said as we passed The Electronic Whip.

'Some place where we can talk. I have a friend . . . uh, another agent working with me in the Park. Should be right down this next street . . . yep, there it is. Hurry, Wicks.'

We sidled along past small concessions. 'There it is, Wicks. The Hareem of the Seven . . . oh damnation and little bananas!'

The string of bulbs over the kootch platform were blacker than my hopes of ever squaring with Goodpasture. A cardboard sign hung crookedly from the platform's edge:

Closed Tonight Only

Just as I was about to weep a few crocodile tears, Wicks lifted the attaché case and wagged it. 'There's a light around back.'

'There is? Let's go see.'

He was correct. At the rear, a dim bulb shed illumination on the asphalt where I had reposed earlier. I bent down near the bottom of the canvas and was about to let out a hiss when the hairs on my neck prickled.

I straightened up. I looked past his shoulder. I mouthed the word, 'Quiet.' I stared at a patch of gloominess further along the alley behind the pitches. For a sec, I would have taken an oath that a human figure had stirred in those shadows.

I waited, my gut wound up tight. A second later, a bedraggled, tough-looking old orange tom cat strolled into the light and gave me the glom with savage green eyes.

'Whew! Just the old imagination working overtime, Wicks. Go on, tabby, beat it. Hiss, hiss.'

I waved my arms and the cat shot off. I bent down again. 'Judy? Are you in there?'

Up went the tent flap. She clapped her hands to her mouth and screeched, 'Johnny!'

'Ssssh!'

I shoved Wicks forward. Moments later, we were inside the wooden-walled dressing cubicle. Wicks' hair hung in his eyes. He looked totally bushed.

'Johnny,' Judy said, 'how did you manage to get away from—?'

'That's another story, Agent Swanson,' I

said, giving her the rolling eyeball and wiggled eyebrow over Wicks' shoulder. 'We needed a place to talk. This is Wicks, Agent Swanson. You remember me talking about Wicks, don't you? Don't you, Agent Swanson?'

'Oh ... oh yes, sure.'

Wicks slumped in a wooden chair. He set his attaché case on the floor. I marched around in front of him, put an authoritative expression on my map and extended my hand.

'Agent Havoc, Wicks. What do the initials stand for? H.T., I mean?'

'You don't know ...' Wicks gulped air, obviously distraught. '... don't know how glad I am to contact you, Havoc. 'This ... whole thing is beginning to drive me out of my mind.' Before I knew it, he'd snapped an engraved card into my hand. The card carried a cartoon logotype showing a merry orangutang swinging from a tree and biting into a big fat sandwich. The type read, HOPPER T. WICKS, Sales Representative, Wunder-Krunch peanut Butter Co., and gave an Industrial Flats address.

'Mr. Wicks,' I said, passing the card, 'is in Peanut butter, Agent Swanson.'

With a total look of bafflement on her charming face, she replied, 'Oh.'

At last I was beginning to unwind slightly. I fired up a weed. 'Just relax, Wicks. Cool

71

off, take it easy. You're in good hands now. I could tell when I discovered you in Stardust Heaven that you were in need of assistance. Sorry we had to cause so much commotion when we ditched the local law people, but you understand how it is with this kind of assignment. You have to treat everybody alike, and that includes the bul—the local police. Not supposed to tip your identity and all that.'

Wicks nodded vehemently. 'Yes, they wouldn't understand at all. They would have thought I was crazy.' His head jerked up. 'But I'm not, Havoc. It's all true.' He patted the initialed attaché case resting beside the chair. 'That's why I've been so careful not to let this out of my sight.'

I tried to restrain my hysterical urge to rip open the case and see what inside could possibly be worth so much floating kale. He continued with slightly narrowed eyes.

'You must have been working with Edson, right? Agent Edson?'

For a moment my befogged thoughts lagged behind my tongue. 'Oh, Agent Edson. Sure. Look here, Wicks.' I tried to put a faint Edward G. timbre in my voice. 'I believe you've been tossing some figures around in public? That wasn't too wise. No, not too wise at all. You see, the ... wrong persons might overhear. Lucky for you that I was on this case. Let's see.' I was practically ready to pass out from expectation. 'I believe the figure you mentioned was ... ah ... in the neighborhood of eight-five thousand dollars?'

'In that neighborhood,' he nodded. I swallowed so loudly, you could have heard it all the way to the Federal Reserve. 'Goddam it, I wouldn't have been in this mess if Lucille hadn't fallen for that lousy floorwax salesman!'

My turn to gargle. 'Lucille? Floorwax salesman? Wicks, you're losing your grip.'

Hopper T. shook his head dolorously. 'Lucille was the girl I was going to marry. She married that floorwax salesman instead. That's why I'm still a bachelor. A salesman with a nice wife, a home ... why, he stays out of trouble. Doesn't hang around bars at all hours. Doesn't get mixed up with cheap, conniving, phony women like Aloha.'

'Aloha?' I said. 'Aloha?'

Had he blown all fuses? Was he re-living an old vacation? Judy Swanson fixed me with a What's-Going-On-Besides-Madness? glance. I shrugged. Wicks never saw it, he was so wound up inside, and babbling half to himself, half to me.

'Yes, Aloha. Aloha, that cheap chippy, that double-timing tramp. Oh, I tell you, Agent Havoc, your line of work may have its dangers, but so does mine. Yes, sir, so does mine. Peanut butter isn't all smooth sailing, not when you meet someone like Aloha.' He

73

raised his head. He looked miserable. 'The hell of it is, Havoc, I'm crazy about her. Absolutely crazy, you understand?'

'Oh, of course, of course,' I said. 'Who is Aloha?'

'It certainly isn't reciprocated though,' he said, continuing to mumble. 'No, not one bit.' Suddenly he leaped up. I was afraid he was going to lunge out into the night, so emotional was he becoming. 'She didn't love me, Havoc. Oh, she said she did, sure. She layed it on thick as Wunder-Krunch Peanut Butter. This thick.' His fingers showed how thick. 'But it was all a flim-flam, a dodge. She conned me. Lied to me. Oh, I tell you, Havoc, she's a fake. What a rotten, deceitful faker!'

Then his anger cooled. His shoulders slumped. He sat down again. 'But I should have expected it. You run into such people when you're a bachelor.'

'Yes, yes,' I murmured. 'Lucille and the floorwax salesman. I understand all that. But listen here, Hopper T. I think we should go back a little. Discuss the contents of that case which you're—'

'I never should have gone to that bar,' he interrupted, one fist smacking into his other palm.

'Bar?'

'Yes, bar. All my trouble started when I went into that bar for a drink. I should have stayed away. But I was lonesome. And it's one of the two places us salesmen here in the South Shore Area hang out when we need a belt after a long day of—'

'Wicks!' I cut in, loud enough to distract him. Vague memories of a roll film salesman capering in the hall outside Kewpie's office filtered into my by-now totally confused pate. That salesman had also mentioned something about two main hangouts for the sundries vendors in the vicinity. 'Wicks, wait a second. Stop alluding to allusions that elude me, will you? Which bar exactly are you talking about? The one at Stardust Heaven?'

Hopper T. shook his head. 'No. That's one of the joints where you're liable to find one of the selling fraternity, all right. But it was the other one I was talking about.'

'Which other one?'

'Why—'

He began making a gesture with his right hand. It was his last act.

I had been bending over Wicks from the right, trying to badger him into some semblance of coherence. Judy had been standing just across the plywood-walled chamber, watching the show with a dazed expression. She was in line to see the door directly, while I only caught the tiny click of the handle, the faint squeak of the hinge from the edges of my so-called mind, just about the split second Hopper T. Wicks, vendor extraordinaire, was lifting his hand to gesture and saying, 'Why—'

Judy screamed and a gun went off.

A powder smell reeked. Poor Wicks opened his eyes to their full size, dropped his jaw, pitched forward on his face with a large, ugly bullet hole in the small of the back of his conservatively striped jacket. He was dead before he hit the floor.

Very suddenly, all my little witticisms and finaglings seemed very cheap and insignificant in front of the abrupt wiping out of the poor guy who had wanted no more than a good sales curve for Wunder-Krunch and a nice home where Lucille would be waiting.

Judy's scream gurgled away, replaced by a gaze of sick horror. She began to chew her right knuckle as the plywood door batted open to the full. A walking bad dream shambled in, cannon first.

It takes longer to tell about him than it did for all the grisly details to sink into my eyeballs and cortex and spell murder. He was tall, ungainly, with outsized shoulders and long, ape-like arms. One of those arms ended in a splay-fingered fist whose fingers were curled around the cannon aimed at Judy and me.

He wore dark slacks, a bedraggled pullover sweat shirt that had once been dark red. His jaw looked to have been broken once or twice. He had a nose like a roll of liverwurst

76

and two dull-witted but menacing eyes. There was a light fuzz of hair still left on his balding, enlarged dome. And when he gave out with a sickly grin that revealed a set of dentures in bad repair, he exuded the scent of cloves.

'I want to talk—' the apparition began.

I had other notions, namely about Judy's safety, and the suddenly valuable attaché case which apparently had the pricetag of the life of Hopper T. Wicks attached.

While the ugly was still talking, I whipped up my right loafer, caught the bottom of the chair in which Wicks had been sitting, kicked hard. The chair sailed into the ugly's gun arm.

'Catch, Judy!' I yelled, pitching her the attaché case. While she caught it, I ripped my keyring out of my pocket and sailed that at her too. It sparkled and jingled toward her in a nice arc, a collection of keys for heap and pad, and a leather tag attached. 'The parking lot—' was all the rest I had time for, before I turned and dove at the pug who was kicking the chair aside and hoisting his cannon.

Beautiful Judy-Salome caught the part of the message about the location of the heap. I butted the bruiser in the belly with my skull, simultaneously giving it to him with both fists. It was like sinking my knuckles into just-hardened concrete. He bopped me on the back of the neck.

I coughed, groaned, dropped to my knees, grabbed outward with both hands. My fingers stuck in something gooey. I caught the rim of the jar, leaped up, dodged the thug's whiplashing arm as he brought the muzzle of the cannon from left to right, attempting to knock my head off my shoulders.

'Run, Judy, for Pete's sake!'

She hesitated, clutching both attaché case and keyring, then darted forward. The bruiser let out a yell, spun as she whizzed past him. He tried to catch her with his free hand. I smashed the object which I had snagged from her dressing table, which was a cold cream jar, over his cranium.

'Damned little—' the bruiser screamed, spinning around again, gobs of cold cream on his skull, ears and neck. I picked up the chair I'd thrown, seized the back, jabbed the legs at him the way lion tamers do. He levelled the cannon. Judy's flying footsteps tapped away, died out.

The bruiser glanced over his shoulder, uncertain as to whether to chase her or handle me. With little homicidal lights in his eyes, he chose the latter. He chuckled low, the clove tang clouding all around as he shoved one sneakered foot forward in a shamble.

'Don't fight me, jerk,' he said through meaty lips. 'Don't pull nothing else because then I'll have to leave you hamburger like that punk on the floor.'

I watched him, saying nothing. A Niagara of sweat cascaded down my back under my Brooks outfit. I kept wondering whether Judy had gotten the message. Whether she'd discover the heap, and see that the address of my pad was printed on cardboard under the cello insert on the leather tag. Whether she'd know enough to go to that address and hide out where she'd be safe, until I discovered who was stirring up the murder soup again.

The ugly made little circling motions with the muzzle of his cannon as he advanced, chuckling and muttering syllables even the Supreme Court would be hard put to defend on grounds of free speech. All I had was the chair. All he had was fourteen tons of overdeveloped muscle, and his cannon, and a plain urge to perforate me with lead tokens of his dislike.

Thrusting the gun ahead suddenly, he made a lunge. I rammed the chair at his midsection, yipped when I went off balance, because I was trying to shove the chair into pure air. The ugly had sidestepped, and now he came at me, from the side. He basted me in the back of the head with the flat of the muzzle. I did the swan routine.

With his foot he rolled me over on my back.

'I ought to put a slug in your Goddam miserable undersized carcass,' he said. 'You fixed it so the twist got away good. Didn't you, huh?'

Scrunch-punch went his toe in my midriff.

'Didn't you, you little creep?' He glanced uneasily at the half open door of the dressing cubicle, listened. 'But we ain't got time for that. Sooner or later, somebody's gonna come runnin' to see about that shot. I guess I got to take you along and be satisfied. Up, junior. Up or I'll put you out and pick you up myself. And I won't do it easy, either.'

I tottered to my shaky feet. 'Why don't you stay around and collect a few medals?' I snarled. 'A bullet in the back for that poor guy lying there. That's a real humane piece of work.'

'Ah, blow it out and get moving.' He gave me a baste in the ribs with the muzzle.

I staggered out through the back of the darkened tent. He shuffled along behind me. The clove tang was unpleasant. 'This way,' he said, when we were outside.

From the park street came a confused babble, as though people weren't sure whether there had been a shot or not. With several shooting galleries going full blast in the vicinity, it would be hard to tell. The ugly shoved me to the left, down past the patch of black from which the orange tom cat had strolled.

'One thing,' I panted. 'You . . . were hiding around here earlier?'

'That's right. That damn pussycat almost

80

gave me away.'

'And ... I bumped into you behind Stardust Heaven. I smelled the clove stink then.'

'Yeah. It's good for the teeth, I read some place. I been lookin' for you, little man. After you beat it out of the dance hall, I asked around. I found out where the milk bottle concession was. There aren't many guys your size around Funnyland, y'know.'

He was growing almost conversational as he hustled me down a maze of dim thoroughfares behind the various tents and concessions. But he missed no chance to whack me in the backbone every few steps to indicate I had better behave.

'I seen the lights were all out in the baseball pitch,' he continued, 'so I prowled around some. That's when I seen the light in that broad's tent, and the sign saying the place was closed. Just then, you and that loudmouth salesman came along. I jumped back in the shadows. After you went in, I snuck inside the tent and listened long enough to find out it was Wicks doin' the talking.' He snapped his fingers. 'Presto. The double-crossing sonofabitch got what he had coming.'

'The executioner,' I growled. 'The very big executioner. Who do you work for?'

'That, my runty friend, you're gonna find out.'

'What's your name?'

'Well, my real name—hell, most people call me Inch. Cause I'm so little, get it?'

I would have laughed except for the fact that, at gunpoint, I might have cried.

CHAPTER SEVEN

Several times during our jaunt down the South Shore Parkway in Inch's crate, which he retrieved from the main Funnyland lot, I debated jumping him. But then I figured I might as well cross my fingers and continue to play the game of Who's Got the Green?

I hadn't been able to see whether Judy Swanson had removed my auto from the lot. The lot was too big. I hoped she had. The point worried me.

I expected Inch to freight us to some out-of-the-way shack or dock house where I would be pulverized still further. Instead, to my surprise, he wheeled it into the asphalt lot in front of a low brick structure with a mess of fake palms planted in front. BAMBOO GROVE, blazed the neon sign ... Polynesian Cuisine.

Inch snagged a sport coat from the back seat, slid the cannon in the side pocket.

'We're goin' in the front way, little man. But don't forget, the pistol's aimed right where you live.'

We entered. Tinny canned Hawaiian music assailed my ears. A waterfall plashed. South Sea masks grinned ghoulishly out of a black nowhere, their cheeks grisly blue. Gradually my optics adjusted. The masks were mounted on the cork walls of the spacious restaurant, and concealed black light spots gave them their eerie luminescence.

The place was already reasonably crowded, with diners enjoying drinks out of coconut shells at small, candle-lit tables. Bold as brass, Inch marched me around the bar, behind which a couple of booze clerks waved cheerily.

'Hiyah, Inch, how goes it?'

He waved back. We rounded the end of the bar, where a lone, horsy-toothed young sergeant in Army dress greens was bent over a double highball on the rocks.

'... dear John letter, by God. And my name isn't John, either. Bartender! Jolt me again.'

Inch hustled me down a hallway, knocked at the door at the end. A peculiarly husky voice said, 'Come in.'

Inch closed the door while I attempted to restrain myself from fainting in horror, or joy, or both.

Horror because no doll-baby this good looking should be mixed up in such a mishmash of mayhem. Joy because no

83

doll-baby this good looking could possibly be part of such doings.

She was so tall—over six feet by at least one inch, I'd bet—she made me look like a toddler. Her hair was dark, glossy, piled very high. Her shoulders were bare and delicious-looking. The scarlet satin gown she wore showed off her positively bountiful bosoms to maximum advantage.

The slinky red gown rustled as she rose, stood smiling while Inch hustled me forward. The cookie regarded me with curiosity and calm, and maybe some amusement. On close examination, I discovered that makeup had not faked those eyes into appearing slightly slanted. The suggestion of almond shape was genuine. Together with her high cheekbones, it indicated she was maybe the only hunk of authentic Polynesian decor in the whole phony layout.

'This guy's name is Havoc, Miss Ross.'

'Aloha Ross,' she said to me, curtly. I remembered the first name, all right. Hopper T. Wicks had said it, with a vengeance. 'I am the hostess as well as the manager of The Bamboo Grove, Havoc. You'll do well to remember that everybody—I repeat, everybody—on the premises will respond instantly to my orders.'

'I'll try to keep that in mind.'

She tapped her long, coral-enameled fingernail on the desk. 'Let's not waste time,

Inch. Where is the case?'

'Well,' Inch gulped, 'the shrimp here tossed it to this broad, y'see...'

Aloha glared. 'In other words you don't have it?'

'Miss Ross, I done the best I could.' He gave a quick account of what had happened. The way the big lug stood quavering, waiting for her reaction, was another measure of how much steel Miss Aloha Ross carried beneath her camouflage of deliciously rounded flesh.

'Very well, Inch. Put on your apron and go back to work behind the bar. I'll deal with our undernourished little friend.'

From his pocket Inch produced the cannon. 'Want me to leave this?'

Her eyes gave me the pin-through-the-butterfly treatment. 'That won't be necessary.'

'It might be,' I said. 'This set-up stinks. It stinks of murder, for one thing.'

Aloha Ross smiled and seated herself in a fanbacked bamboo chair behind the desk. Inch departed. Aloha made sure I got a provocative flash of her leggy goodies as she crossed her knees. While I stood like a mope on the fiber carpet, she fitted a long cigarette into a longer ivory holder and lit up.

'Havoc is your name? You have a rather pushy personality for one so small.'

'Yeah, well, I'm not the only one who'll be pushing. The cops will be, when they learn—'

'The police will learn nothing dear,' she interrupted. 'Remember where you are. Now, where is the girl to whom you gave the attaché case?'

I almost laughed. Almost. The piled hairdo, the Oriental-Occidental features, the cigarette holder all shouted fakeroo, like the decorations of the Bamboo Grove. Only the hard, confident merriment in her eyes told me the broad was real trouble.

'Girl?' I said. 'Attaché case?'

She suppressed irritation. 'What is the girl's name, dear?'

'Name? Whose name?'

'Very well. Let's try another tack. Are you a government agent?'

Now I was getting somewhere. She couldn't quite conceal the edginess behind the query. Everything in the game was against me; I wasn't even sure I knew the nature of the game itself. But there were eighty-five thousand loose bucks involved somewhere, and I wanted to discover where. I also had hopes of pinning the vicious bulleting of Hopper T. Wicks on Miss Aloha Ross's lovely front porch.

'That's right,' I said. 'I am a federal agent. Or am I? Why don't you figure it out?'

'Mr. Havoc, you exasperate ...' She stopped, shook her head. She rose slowly from behind the desk. She smoothed her

86

gown over her amply rounded hips. Slowly she came around the corner of that desk, looking taller, the closer she got. Soon my neck had a crick in it.

As is usual with tall cookies, her bust line was on a level with my nose. As she bent over, the bodice of her scarlet dress offered me new scenic views. She tickled my left cheek with her long fingernails.

'You're a peculiar little man. Rather good looking, in a rascally sort of way. I've never ... ah ... encountered a man of your precise size. It might be fun, don't you think?'

What 'might be fun,' her glance said explicitly.

I struggled manfully to keep my hormones under control as she went tickle, tickle, tickle with her nails along my hairline and laughed in a husky voice. To further tantalize, she leaned close, puckered for a kiss.

It took all the strength at my disposal to resist the clamor of my ductless glands and say, 'Go smooch with somebody else, baby. A little lipstick isn't a high enough price by half.'

She straightened up, angry. 'My, you're a difficult little bastard.'

'You haven't discovered how difficult.'

As she stood scrutinizing me, I was already doing mental leapfrog to the next gambit. A bluff could certainly get me in no additional difficulty.

'Let me specify the details for you, Miss Ross. I am a free agent.'

'Now we're getting somewhere.'

'Just hang on. Some people call me a hustler. I say I'm interested in my welfare first. I am not working for anybody except yours truly, J. Havoc. And, I want a split.'

Aloha's right eyebrow hooked up. 'A split? Whatever do you mean?'

'Don't give me the stupidity routine. You know what I'm talking about.' She had to, because I certainly didn't. 'Besides, I've got the leverage to get it. Hopper T. Wicks is dead. And ...' (bluffing wild again) '... and so is Mr. Edson. And we know who was responsible for both, don't we?'

She laughed, one hundred per cent pure ice. 'Not I, dear little man. It was Inch. I might add that he could perform the same function where you are concerned, if you become more troublesome than you already are.'

'I won't stop being troublesome 'till we cut the cake.'

For a moment, I sorted out the various implications of her reply. On a wild flyer, I had handed her Edson's corpse. I wasn't sure whether she had acknowledged it along with that of Wicks, but from the naked, pitiless way she lamped me, I suspected she had. She shrugged. She revolved neatly on one heel, returned to the desk.

88

Reposing in the bamboo chair once again, she was all business. 'Why must we haggle, Mr. Havoc? If you are an ... ah ... independent businessman, what is your interest in this matter? Of what possible good could that collection of scandalous and indiscreet letters be to you?'

'Letters?' I mumbled.

'It's quite simple. That poor man Hopper Wicks was in love with me. He wrote me letters. Incriminating, damaging letters. Indiscreet letters which he wanted back, because he was afraid his wife might see them. I will admit his death was regrettable, but he was causing me a great deal of trouble. Now do you see why ... ?' Suddenly her gaze blackened. 'What in hell do you find so funny, Mr. Havoc?'

'You,' I snorted. 'This whole rotten routine. Letters worth eighty-five grand? And the lives of two men, one of them a government agent? I may look underfed, Miss Ross, but my brains get their full quota of vitamins, thanks a lot. How dumb do you think I am? I know Hopper Wicks was a bachelor and so do you.'

That rocked her.

'All right, Havoc. How much else do you know?'

'Lots,' said I, smugly.

'Listen, you filthy little ...' She controlled herself. 'You must be more specific than "lots."'

'Specific enough to ask for—and get—a 50 percent split of any and all monies involved, baby.'

'Fifty percent!' The glaciers in her eyes froze even thicker. 'I'm sorry, Havoc. I think you're lying. I won't play. What I plan to do instead is call for Inch. I think he can force you to reveal exactly how much you know. Even if he does have to pry it out of you one bloody little bit at a time.'

And one of her long-nailed fingers swept across the desk to a call box studded with buttons.

But before she could summon him, he arrived. He bammed the door and rushed in, now wearing a white shirt, clip-on bow tie and bar apron.

'Miss Ross! We got a mess outside.'

Her temper uncorked. 'Handle it yourself, you dimwit.'

Inch blinked. 'Okay. But ... you like to keep on good terms with the sojer boys, so I thought ...' He stopped, looking dismayed and distinctly un-bright.

'Trouble with someone from Fort Parnell, is it?' Her whole manner had changed.

Big Inch nodded. 'There was this sergeant at the bar, see. Well, his girl sent him this here Dear John letter, and he was saucing up because of it. He got kind of rowdy and took a swing at one of the waiters who tried to cool

90

him down.'

'Did you call the MPs from the Fort?'

'Sure. That's what I come to tell you. They're awready here to take him away.'

Aloha smoothed her gown again. 'Very good, Inch. I'm sorry I lost my temper. You did precisely right. I'll go out and talk to them.'

And she sailed past, trailing clouds of some exotic scent. 'You see, Mr. Havoc,' she said mockingly, 'I have a fine reputation for cooperating with the local military when one of the soldiers happens to get out of hand. I wouldn't want to spoil that. Inch! Watch him. I'll be back in a few seconds.'

The door shut. That's when I made up my mind to risk all. I could see nothing at the end of a more prolonged visit with Miss Ross except my corpse laid out in some drainage ditch some place. Before Inch could even gather his assorted wits to issue instructions to me, I snatched a big oyster shell ashtray off the desk and let fly.

'You damned—!' he shouted, just as the sharp edge of the shell caught him in the snout.

I was right behind it. I didn't play it the gentlemanly way. I bopped him in the gut with both fists, then gave him a knee in the personal possessions.

'Ow, you lousy little schmuck ... I'll kill you!'

91

'Got to catch me first,' I panted, eluding his outstretched hands and racing into the corridor.

I was greeted by a friendly little tableau upon arriving in the bar area. Aloha was chatting with a pair of chunky, rough-looking MPs with the usual white helmets, arm bands and swagger sticks. A foot or so beyond them, waiting mopishly, was the horse-toothed sergeant, wavering in intoxication.

Aloha turned curiously to see who was making the racket. Her cordial smile hardened like quick-set cement as I charged past.

'Let me out of here, stand aside, you miserable storm troopers!' cried I, and took a swing at the first MP.

The swing was harder than I'd planned. He grabbed his nasal region and caromed against the bar. Immediately the other MP laid hands on me, raising his swagger stick with menace.

'Just a minute, fellah! Accosting a military policeman is—'

'Get your hands off me!' I squealed, flailing my arms but not trying to hit anybody. The MP was strong. He collared me without much difficulty. The other MP righted himself and rubbed his reddened schnozz.

'Stand still before I smack you!' the MP yelled. Diners at the tables stared. I hoped it looked like the upraised stick had cowed me. 'That's better,' the MP muttered. 'Well, Miss

Ross, this looks like another customer you'll want to get rid of.'

Aloha's temper was simmering. She sensed the ploy. 'Why, Corporal, he's just a . . . just a cheap drunk. I'll be glad to call the police for you. Leave him with me.'

The MP I'd pasted shook his head. 'Sorry, Miss Ross. He may be a civilian, and we'll have to turn him over to the civilian cops eventually. But we have to do the reporting when he assaults a man in uniform. We'll take him along to the Fort and file the complaint from there. Thanks for your cooperation, by the way.'

'Oh,' she said, fixing me with visual daggers, 'oh, of course. Don't mention it.'

The first MP prodded me with his stick. 'Come on, loony. You're going to get a nice trip to the Fort. And from there to the pokey.'

'Anything you say,' I wheezed. 'I guess I had it coming.'

They shoved me around and pushed me along. I almost expected Aloha Ross to let me have a cocktail fork or something in the back. But all she could do was glare venom. The MPs and I exited from The Bamboo Grove and marched toward the flagged jeep parked in the lot.

I was delighted to be temporarily free of the lethal Miss Aloha. But I was not so sure I wanted to be in the hands of the military. Out

93

of the pan, as they say, spang on my pratt in the frying flames.

CHAPTER EIGHT

The MPs piled the horse-toothed sergeant and me into the back seat of the jeep, then peeled rubber and zipped off down the highway. I held onto my porkpie as the wind whistled over the windshield.

Rousing himself from his misery, the sergeant tugged at my sleeve. 'Hey. Hey, buddy.'

'I'm not your buddy. I'm guilty enough without guilt by association.'

'Look,' he said, somewhat more soberly, 'I'm sorry as hell you're in a jam. I ... I gotta thank you for taking a little of the heat off me.' He extended a paw. Reluctantly, I shook. His eyes lit up. 'The name's Zupanzic. Sergeant Herman Zupanzic, put her there.'

'What do they do to civilians who slug MPs, Zupanzic?'

The MP who wasn't driving turned and went, 'Hah!'

Zupanzic leaned over and said under his breath, 'Listen, I'll help you if I can. I mean, I'll keep an eye open and see whether—'

'Pipe down,' came the bark from the front.

I nearly lost my fillings when the driver

spun the wheel and sent the jeep racing down an asphalt feeder road that branched away from the shore. To the left, the Funnyland lights were screened behind trees. Woods closed in close about the road. Up ahead, a few lights twinkled. The jeep stopped outside a barbed wire fence. Half a dozen uniformed guards with machine guns were on duty. They all looked like tough apples, wore paratroop boots and funny green berets. Over the gates hung a sign:

Fort Percy Parnell

Authorized Personnel

ONLY

'Tonight the tea rose fell off the bush,' said the MP driving.

'Yeah,' said the tallest guard, 'and the grub worms are eating the lawn.'

'But the fertilizer will give them indigestion,' said the driver.

'Proceed.'

The driver touched his helmet. A motor whined, the gate slid aside and the jeep gunned. As we shot down a long street between darkened barracks, I whispered to Zupanzic, 'Say, what in cripes do you guys do that makes all that secret rigamarole necessary?'

'Oh,' he said vaguely, 'just, uh, military work.'

'I'd never have guessed. By the way, who the hell was Percy Parnell? Some general?'

Zupanzic blinked. 'We've been trying to find out for years. If you find out, let me know.'

The MPs pulled up beside a lighted building, held a short discourse, the burden of which was that, as it was now almost two o'clock in the morning—0200 in their jargon—they might as well hold me overnight until General Bark came on duty in the a.m. Thus I was hustled into the building and locked in a room with wire mesh over the windows.

I paced round and round the cubicle, worrying. Judy Swanson—was she O.K.? I hoped like crazy that she had gotten safely to my pad.

Toward 0400, Sergeant Zupanzic showed up with a tray of chow. I gathered he was doing me a favor until I looked at the cream chip beef on toast. I managed to eat a little, and even snooze. I woke up around seven o'clock. Companies of tough apples in paratroop boots and green berets were hup-hupping in the street outside. The sun was shining. A jeep load of reasonably good looking WACs buzzed by the window. Altogether, it looked like a swell day for my execution.

The door banged open shortly after 0800. 'General wants to see you, buddy,' said the guard. 'Old Cement-Schnozz Bark himself. You must be in big trouble.'

They marched me out, three on either side. I felt like some kind of traitor, the way they kept their machine guns poised. We walked the equivalent of two blocks down the street, turned in at a large, two-story barracks-type building, passed through an outer office where several trim WACs were already working at files and typewriters in a bullpen. The head guard knocked on a door whose nameplate read, Maj. Gen. Morris B. Bark, Commandant.

'Come,' Bark barked. I was thrust into the Presence.

'Oh, good morning, good morning, my little friend,' said Detective Goodpasture.

'Fitz! What the hell are you doing here?'

'No cursing on this base, Goddam it,' cried another voice.

General Morris B. Bark was a fiftyish type, stocky, but not with an ounce of fat. His eyes beneath thick tufts of graying brows had all the sweet, human, emotional warmth of twelve-inch stove bolts.

'So,' he said. 'You are Mr. Havoc. The civilian who assaulted one of our military policemen.'

'But now,' said Goodpasture with fiendish pleasure as he worked his moist cigar in his glum mouth, 'it looks bigger than that, eh, General?'

'Yes,' said Bark, 'it certainly does. As if I haven't got enough pains in the a—trouble.'

97

'Goodpasture,' I said, 'for once I'm glad to see you. I can explain to you and the General why I had to slug that guy. You see, this dame wanted—'

'Speak when you're spoken to!' Bark roared.

'Come on, General! I'm not one of your laddies in uniform, remember. I happen to be the taxpayer who helps freight your salary. Listen, Goodpasture, help me out!'

'I'll help you out,' he said. 'Oh, yes, will I help you out! Headquarters woke me out of a sound sleep. You know, because of my standing watch for your name, John. General Bark's MPs telephoned headquarters early this morning. Civil Police matter, y'know. I rushed right over. You can imagine how sad I was to learn you were in more trouble. I'm not forgetting how you made fools of me and my men last night at Funnyland.'

General Bark stood behind his desk, parade-rest style, owling me. 'Your name is Havoc?'

Before I could open my map, Goodpasture broke in: 'General, one second. You know his name is Havoc. What you may not know is that he is already in several very substantial jams. Including—' (gleefully he ticked them off on his fingers), '—two suspicions of homicide, and associating with persons suspected of being foreign agents. As you also know, this entire affair goes a lot deeper than

98

even I am aware of. The civil police have been running interference to keep you gentlemen of the military in the background. I confess I don't know the full score. I'd like you to tell me as much as you can without violating security. I think you've got my clearance there somewhere...'

He gestured to a pile of papers on the desk. Bark picked one up. 'Hmmm, yes. It's Triple AAA, Blue Streak, All Classes Except For Your Eyeballs Only.'

'Well,' said the Detective, 'if that's the case, you can paint in some of the details? Then I'll be in a better position to deal with Havoc here. Charge him with every last possible charge we can make stick. Can you do that for me, General?'

'Affirmative! But not with him listening. Orderly!'

Who should waltz in but a weary and hangdog Sgt. Zupanzic.

'Yes, sir?'

'Lock this little ... gentleman in Colonel Cooper's office next door until I send for him.'

As Zupanzic led me to my improvised cell, he whispered cheerfully: 'Really letting you have it, huh? Too bad, too bad. Well, just let me know what I can do. Within reason, of course.'

'Thanks an oversized heap,' I said wearily as the door slammed. The lock clicked.

I glanced around the office. It was about half the size of Bark's. I rued the fact that I might be missing some of the vital pieces of the eighty-five thousand clam puzzle. Then, all at once, my eyes lit on the heat register down by the floorboards, in the wall between this office and Bark's.

If anybody looked in the window, I was cooked. But I took the chance. It was one time when it was an advantage to be of miniature size.

I pried the cover off the heat run and inserted the upper half of my person in the wall, with my legs sticking out into the office. From this novel position, I could see a faint gleam of light around a bend in the sheet metal. Mercifully, it was spring, not winter, so I got no scalding air in the puss. I heard a voice weakly but clearly:

'Do you know anything about the function of Fort Parnell, Detective?'

'No, I mean negative, General.'

'Well, Detective, Fort Parnell is H.Q. for the Second Special Assault Division. We're a special services outfit. Guerilla and psychological warfare. We train to handle bushfire actions wherever they might break out. You can tell we're special services, incidentally, from those green berets the lads wear. Those berets raise hell in public, I might say. Why, more than once, some fool yelling, 'Yoo-hoo, soldier, where'd you get

100

the pretty hat?' or something equally insulting has touched off a riot. The boys in the 2nd S.A.D. are very sensitive.'

'Remind me never to whistle at one of them, heh-heh,' said Fitz fatuously.

'Yes, for your own protection. Well, naturally, we here at Fort Parnell are just one more target for foreign espionage apparati, if that's the plural for apparatus. Everybody's in the spying business these days. Trying to learn the composition of the 2nd S.A.D., what our strength is, so forth and so on. A few months back, some agents working for the C.I.A. picked up some very specific data about Fort Parnell, in Hong Kong. The material was on its way to the Red Chinese. Nothing really damaging the first time, thank God. But it definitely indicated a leak.'

'A leak around here? All the way to China? That's a long leak, General.'

'Affirmative. Well, we had investigators up from Washington, of course. They concluded that one point of leakage might be that damn amusement park, Funnyland. At minimum, it was the place my lads were always getting into trouble because of their berets. First, we declared the Park off limits. Then counter-intelligence planted an operative in a gang run by an unsavory punk named Kewpie North. North's bunch—not as security risks, mind you; as hoodlums— supposedly had a line on most of the shady

101

affairs in the neighborhood. The operative's name was Edson.'

Goodpasture did vocal flipflops. 'Edson! But he's been murdered.'

'Affirmative. Which makes for a hell of a mess. Yes, sir, a hell of a mess. For one thing, we're getting ready for war games today. They start tomorrow, Saturday, in that big stretch of woods over that way. And as if I don't have enough on my mind with this Edson business, and now this other dead man—Wicks?—you mentioned earlier, I'm going to be saddled with an inspector from the Joint Chiefs. He's coming to look at the maneuvers. General D. D. Offenbach.'

'Drum-Drum Offenbach? The one who said he'd run his tanks over his own grandmother if it would win a war?'

'That's right. He's a real fire-breather.'

Some of this floated around in my head in a half-baked way as I lay supine in the heat run with my map pasted against sheet metal. I was thinking also about Aloha Ross.

No wonder the sneaky, sexy bim was working so hard to preserve the spirit of 'fine cooperation' with the MPs from the Fort. Secret Agent Edson might have suspected her of spy shenanigans, but since her name hadn't come up thus far, it was clear Bark didn't.

Another fact was also compellingly clear:

Something in the possession of Hopper T. Wicks—something reposing within that black attaché case—was worth at least eighty-five thousand smackeroos on the Hot Intelligence Market.

And Judy had the attaché case.

And ... where was Judy?

While the parties in the next office mumbled about what steps to take next, I squeaked back out of the heat run, forced the cover in place and conducted a vigorous mental debate with myself.

Should I give Goodpasture the word and let him move in on Aloha Ross?

Yes, that was probably the best way.

Except that Goodpasture, the rat, had given me such a hard time so often before. My dishonest instincts rebelled.

Look at it this way, I said to myself. You are in over your sometimes swelled head, true. And it may be unpatriotic, true. Also counter to national security, true.

But did I want to fix Aloha Ross personally? Or did I want to let the bureaucrats do it? And did I want to fix Inch too? And did I want eighty-five thousand clams? Did I want all those things, unpatriotic hustler that I was?

Of course I did.

'Hey, Havoc.' It was Zupanzic again. 'The General wants you.'

Once in the office, with my pair of oppressors glowering, I smiled blandly and said, 'Yes, boys?'

103

Bark said, 'Havoc, now that you've had time to think it over, what do you want?'

'Nothing. Except that I demand my constitutional rights. Namely, one telephone call to my lawyer.'

Detective First Grade Goodpasture shook a finger. 'Havoc, you're a fine one to talk about constitutional rights. You, with your bending, breaking and flouting of the law whenever it suits you! I warn you, Havoc, this time you're out of your depth.'

I had a poignant feeling he was right. But I said, 'Where's the phone?'

General Bark and Goodpasture conferred in whispers. Neither was pleased about this development. I kept prodding. 'Come on, come on. Do I get to make the call or do I start hollering?'

'Affirmative. I mean negative!' Bark flushed.

He called for Sergeant Zupanzic again. Zupanzic conducted me back to Colonel Cooper's cell. I slammed the door, picked up the phone and started to dial. I heard heavy breathing.

'Kindly get off the extension, boys,' I said.

Whoever it was hung up. I dialed the number of my pad in the city. The phone went *brrrring* and *brrrring* and my heart began to fall down to my arches when no one—

'Hello?'

'Judy? Judy, is that you?'

'I'm afraid you have the wrong number, sir,' she said.

'Wait, wait, I do not!' I howled. 'Judy, this is John Havoc, J. Havoc, in person.'

'Johnny! Where are you?'

'In trouble.'

'I've been waiting here for hours. I figured when you threw me the keys you wanted me to come here, but I thought you'd show up soon after. Are you all right?'

'I'm not positive. Listen, have you got that attaché case?'

'Of course. Johnny, who was that awful, hideous man who shot—?'

'Never mind, I'll explain later. And look, for God's sake, honey, don't call the police this time. They're already ... I mean, you haven't called them, have you?'

'No, not after what happened when I called them before.'

I mopped my brow. 'Good. Now quick. Look in the attaché case and tell me—'

'I already have looked in it. Johnny, it's just a lot of junk.'

'Junk?' I goggled at the mouthpiece. Two men shot, and it was junk? 'Judy, that can't be.'

'Silly stuff,' she said. 'Reports all typed out on how many cases of Wunder-Krunch Peanut Butter were sold to the commissary at some place called Fort Parnell, and how many tubes of toothpaste were sold, and how many rolls of film to the PX and ... Johnny? Are you there?'

I was there, but I was numb.

My God! Hopper T. Wicks had been a madman. A flippo case. Judy was right, the contents of the attaché case did sound worthless. Peanut butter sales figures, for criminey's sake!

Then all the sweat for the eighty-five thousand clams was for naught. Those rolls and rolls of dollar bills were idle fancies.

I swallowed hard, said, 'Okay, Judy, I guess—'

Across the wire came a long, chilling scream.

Judy's.

'Judy? Judy! My God, what happened? Judy, are you okay? Honey! Answer!'

Click-o. The line went dead.

I jiggled the bar until the dreadful thought penetrated. Whether there was junk in that attaché case or not, someone thought the case contained the real goods.

Someone who had just taken over possession of the case. And poor Judy Swanson with it.

And here I was, Bungler Havoc, with barbed wire, soldiers, the law, the government, and a whole mess of miles between me and any chance in hell of helping her.

CHAPTER NINE

For a minute, I could do nothing except gawp at the receiver in my shaking hand. Visions of Judy Swanson being subjected to all sorts of unwholesome mayhem flitted through my head.

A shadow flickered across the frosted glass of the door. I hung up the phone loudly, wondering how much General Bark's minion had heard. I opened the door.

'Okay,' I said, 'take me back to the torture chamber.'

'Did you get you lawyer okay?' Zupanzic asked.

'Uh, things didn't work out so well,' I replied with a vague stare. 'That's why I may need your help, buddy.'

'W-w-wait a sec!' he said. 'I mean, you took the heat off me, okay. All I got from the CO was a reprimand once I explained about my girlfriend kissing me off. But I didn't figure you'd be mixed up with the General personally when I offered to help. I mean, Bark's a real iron-ass. If he catches me doing anything out of line—'

'Oh,' I said. 'I see. You're a welsher, huh?'

'No! I'll help you. I mean, if I won't get into more trouble.'

'That's big of you.'

'I don't want to go to the stockade. I'm a career man.'

'Right. And as of this moment, your career consists of waiting for a signal from me. Clear? Clear. Now quit jawing.' I raised my voice. 'Okay, okay, Sarge, quit shoving! I'll go quietly.' And I hurled myself through the door of the commandant's office.

FitzHugh Goodpasture sat in a chair, his moist cigar rotating in his glum mouth. General Bark turned from the window.

'You've got a bunch of storm troopers around here,' I said, dusting off my lapels.

'Glad to see the sergeant is on the ball,' said Bark. 'We can't afford to take chances with someone of your caliber. The detective here has filled me in on your exploits.'

'Thanks a ton, FitzHugh.'

He bobbed his head. 'My pleasure. What did your lawyer say?'

'I ... uh ... wasn't able to persuade him to touch this deal,' I hedged. In a way, since I hadn't called him, it was true.

FitzHugh chuckled. 'You have a very smart lawyer, John.'

Through this, I kept seeing Judy Swanson's face. Her mouth suddenly covered up by somebody's meaty paw as they jerked her off the phone. I had to get out of this place. I absolutely had to. To try and hand them an honest explanation would be futile. Goodpasture would hee-haw, and Bark was solidly on his side. Like it or not, I was forced to continue to play the independent.

Outside the window, a large green-painted truck loaded with refuse cans buzzed by in the Fort street. Several WACs walked along. I kept thinking of that barbed wire fence. I not only had to get out of this office, I had to escape from the Fort and over that damned fence. Some problem.

Goodpasture gave Bark the significant fish-eye. 'General, I believe I should hold a further consultation with Washington by telephone.'

'Very well. I can handle this little ... gentleman, don't worry.'

He had nothing to handle. I sat morosely while Goodpasture went out. He returned shortly, flushed,

'They want me down in Washington right away, General. With Havoc along. They suggest I fly down.' He fixed me with a malevolent eye. 'This time, John, you will be questioned by experts.'

He started to work out the details with the general. I entertained visions of myself a prisoner forever in the secret catacombs of the Pentagon. Bark was nodding. He reached for the phone, said as he dialed:

'... will take a load off my mind, frankly. I'm glad to have the whole mess in Washington's lap. Especially with our war games beginning tomorrow, and General

109

Offenbach flying in to inspect for the Joint Chiefs. We have an airstrip here, by the way. I can arrange ...' He paused, listened, put down the horn. 'Busy. Well, we can stroll down the hall to the Logistics Staff Room and check personally. If one of our transports is on the line this morning, I can have you flown to Washington directly from here.'

'I'm all for that,' said FitzHugh. 'The fewer chances that little hustler has to escape, the happier I'll be.'

'Orderly!' The horse-toothed Sergeant Zupanzic appeared. Bark told him to watch me while he and FitzHugh went out. As soon as they were gone, I said:

'O.K., old buddy. This is where you pay off. I'm going out that window.'

Zupanzic's color resembled that of skim milk. 'You're off your nut. You can't get away.'

'Leave that to me,' I said, though he was probably right. 'When I give the word, you let out a big howl, like I slugged you. When somebody comes, tell 'em I went—let's see—to the left, out that window. I'll take off the other way. All I want is half a minute's head start.'

'I'll be court martialed,' he wailed.

'Now, now, that's a good lad. Do your duty.'

I scuttled to the open window, peeked out. The Fort street seemed relatively deserted,

110

except for a platoon of tough apples in their para boots and green berets marching off somewhere, about two blocks on my left. I poised for the jump over the sill.

'Okay, Zupanzic. Start hollering. Roll around on the floor like you've been creamed. Up the rebels!'

And out I went.

I took off like a bat down the Fort street. There was no point in trying a casual stroll. In my Brooks rig, nobody would mistake me for a member of the Armed Forces, ever. From Bark's office window a yell arose.

I zipped past one barracks, another, approached a cross street. So far, a piece of cake. A jeep swung around the corner.

The officer riding with the noncom driver did a double take, leaped up, grabbed for his side-arm.

'Stop! Stop, you ... you civilian, there! Let me see your permission to...'

'Here's my permission!' cried I, picking up a litter can reposing on the porch of a barracks and sailing it through the air at the vehicle.

The litter can struck the jeep hood, knocked the windshield loose from its mounting posts and sent its metal edge slamming back to crack the poor noncom driver in the jaw. The surprise caused him to step on the gas. The jeep shot forward into the side of the barracks, where it produced a large crash and a larger hole.

Both soldiers were climbing out from a mess of lath, plaster and siding as I went pelting away.

A whistle blasted. I craned around. The officer and the noncom had been joined by FitzHugh Goodpasture and General Bark. I ran like crazy, whipping past another barracks building, another. Up ahead, the street came to a dead end at the barbed wire fence. Beyond, trees and fields could be seen. I screwed my head around again, saw that my pursuit now included a trio of MPs waving billy-sticks.

Time for a change of tactics.

There were only two or three wooden buildings left on the street, so I picked the first one, zipped up the steps and in the door without bothering to look at anything else. I whipped down a hall, at the end of which I glimpsed a large, empty barracks with a set of double doors at the far end. One or two soldiers in peculiar uniforms were moving about behind a couple of double bunks, I noticed.

Other sounds registered. Namely, a sort of wet hissing and a chicken-like clucking. Female clucking.

I nearly fell over in a faint as a door at one side of the hall slapped open and two broads came out. One was a shapely redhead, the other was a two hundred fifty-pound fatty.

112

Both were one hundred percent naked except for khaki towels which they clutched to their damp persons.

'... and I told the Lieutenant,' Beefy was saying, 'I said, Lieutenant, if I am going to stay in the service, I am going to stay in the way I am. Namely, pleasingly plump. And if the Lieutenant doesn't like it, the Lieutenant can take it and s—a man!'

The redhead threw up her hands. The khaki towel dropped. 'My God! A man!'

'Just a hallucination,' I cried, attempting to rush on. But before I knew it, half a dozen other totally naked janes were crowding the hall, all screaming and hollering and trying to smack me.

'Wait, wait!' I exclaimed. 'Let me go! I'm just a ... uh, brush salesman. I got lost. Which way to the PX?'

Horribly, I realized I had stumbled into a barracks occupied by some of those WACs on the base. The peculiar pale-uniformed soldiers in the barracks proper weren't uniformed soldiers at all, but broads in various stages of undress.

The beefy WAC flung an elbow around my windpipe. 'Hold him, girls! Hold the little rat—'

'No, no,' I panted, struggling to extricate myself from a tangle of slippery thighs and bosoms. 'I'm a salesman!'

'I've always said the salesmen they let on

113

this base are sex maniacs,' another jane cried.

Round and round my head one of the broads wrapped her wet towel. Frantically I tried to tear it off. Some of the bimbos screamed like they'd sighted mice and others cursed like troopers. Soon I was down on my knees and trying to crawl away from them, which was difficult as I had the towel around my head and couldn't see.

'Grab him, Helga, he's trying to get away!' came a distant outcry.

'I hate to do this,' I said, and pinched something.

'Oooo, the little bastard bit me on the knee!' a WAC cried.

With a kick or two, I suddenly burst through the tangle of legs and, panting, regained my feet. Through the forest of bouncing bosoms and behinds, I saw the barracks door crash open while I frantically unwrapped the towel from my cranium. I glimpsed the outthrust jaw of General Bark, the spaniel puss of Goodpasture.

'Ten-hut!' cried I.

Military training is the nuts. All the janes went to attention, and towels fluttered down. Goodpasture reeled against the wall, near to fainting. Bark turned fourteen shades of red, shouted:

'As you were! I mean ... at ease ... I mean ... Goddam it, cover up! We're looking for—'

114

'There he goes!' a WAC cried. And there I went.

The WACs in the barracks proper started to shriek and yowl as loudly as the dames from the shower room. Bark was howling. 'MPs, MPs forward! Get these broa—get these women out of the way! Catch that man!'

One of the WACs in the hall went really hysterical: 'The General's gone berserk! It's a rape! Oh, girls, it's a mass rape—'

'Oooooo!'

'Help, help!'

'Mass rape, mass rape!'

'Save us, save us...'

As I whizzed through the barracks room, several WACs in panties, bras, both or nothing at all began peeping out from behind their beds. They yanked off their blankets and tossed them into the aisle. I managed to jump over most of them, spreading consternation as I ran by shouting, 'Watch out, girls, watch out! They forgot to put that chemical in the mashed potatoes. The General's gone berserk! Hed—whoops!'

My own brogans got all tangled in one of the tossed blankets. Before I knew it, I was flat on my butt on the floorboards while two totally naked WACs leaped on my midsection.

'Hold him down, Florence! Hold the little rapist down so he can't move.'

'Coming through, coming through!'

Goodpasture was screaming, fighting his way out of the hall. My two captors bounced up and down on me, using their bare behinds to knock my wind to hell and gone. They were expert at it. *Bounce, bounce, bounce.* I wiggled, I writhed. There was no way out—except one.

I pinched both bottoms simultaneously.

'Ohhhh!' shrieked the jane sitting on my lower stomach, skyrocketing up.

'Watch it, grandmother,' yelled I, upsetting the other chick. Off balance, she went dancing and cavorting down the aisle and landed with a smack against General Bark. I ran for the double doors again while the noise grew even more fearful.

I banged my ankle against an open foot locker, reached down, scooped up several handfuls of items I found neatly folded there. Whirling, I began to throw these items with all my might.

Whap, wham, whizzo! Still tussling with the naked WAC, General Bark got a pair of briefs over his ear and a bra across his forehead. 'Have some undies, FitzHugh!' I yelped, and let fly with another salvo.

Zip, zap, zowie! I pitched briefs and bras at the pursuers until the air was thick with flying unmentionables. The MPs got tangled up in shoulder straps and D-cups and what have you. An MP hit a WAC on the noggin with his billystick by accident, the jane

116

responded with personal self defense and gave him a good old-fashioned knee lift. This doubled the guy on the floor. Fighting and struggling with the WAC, and still with undergarments obscuring his vision, General Bark tripped over the MP. The WAC went down in the fracas, too, screaming like a fire siren:

'Rapist, rapist, rapist!'

'Negative, negative, negative!' Bark cried, under a fast-mounting mountain of tripping bodies and raining undergarments.

'I'll fix you, you dirty old man!' another WAC howled, and gave Goodpasture the palm of her hand under the chin. Her aim was off just a mite. His cigar was flattened against his map.

Panting, my tie askew, my hat barely hanging on my head, I crashed against the double doors, pulled them open and rushed outside.

The barbed wire fence reared up ahead of me. But down at the building's corner, I saw the back end of a parked military refuse truck. I raced that way, while the cries, screams, moans, curses, howls and other assorted noises of a riot in progress split the morning air.

In a trice I was into the truck's cab. Someone had left the keys, thank God. I kicked the engine over, jerked the floor shift into reverse and backed the wagon at the barbed wire full tilt.

There was a wrench, a cracking, and the truck stalled. Out I went like a shot.

The truck's tailgate had whammed a large dent on the chain link. I squeezed between the top strands of barbed wire and the mashed-down fence proper and started running like crazy through the weeds.

Directly ahead, thick woodlands waited. I reached the sanctuary of the trees, panting. I turned. On the other side of the fence, the riot spilled into the open.

General Bark was expostulating with a group of WACs. To no avail. They let him have it over the noggin with hot water bottles and he sailed through the air. Goodpasture reeled outside, his clothes in shreds. The screaming and yelling was horrendous.

Well, Havoc, nothing could be worse, so why wait around? I didn't.

I turned my back on the madness and took off through the thick woods. Soon I left the woods and was in an open field, where a couple of menacing looking Army tanks were parked, unattended. Ready for tomorrow's war games? In truth, we had already had the war games back in the WAC barracks.

But when they caught me again, the word games would hardly apply. My little games might get me locked up for life.

I raced around the tanks and kept running.

CHAPTER TEN

Uphill and down dale, where the ragweed and the crabgrass bloomed, I hoofed along for the better part of two hours. Finally, covered with dust and depressed by a feeling of total exhaustion and frustration, I scrambled up to the crest of a brush-covered hill and there, gleaming in all its hokey grandeur, I saw the sprawl of Funnyland Park.

I sat down under a tree and smoked my first butt since bugging the Fort. If Goodpasture and Bark had put trackers on my trail, which I assumed they had, I had eluded them by dumb luck alone. Now, though I had a dozen problems hanging fire, my main one was Judy.

Presently I began a limping dogtrot toward the Park. Lights began to wink in the dusk. I had spent most of the afternoon afoot. By the time I reached the main parking area, night was setting in. My car was gone, all right. I headed for a cab stand at the Park's main entrance.

The hack driver tooled us down the highway. First stop, The Bamboo Grove.

Even before we got within reading distance of the neon, you could tell the sign was blacked out. The lot was empty. We swung around past the entrance. A big placard had

119

been tacked up. CLOSED UNTIL FURTHER NOTICE.

'Where to now, buddy?'

'Back down the road. That public phone booth we passed.'

That the Grove was closed gave me a small sense of satisfaction. Perhaps my antics had not been altogether useless. Aloha was running scared. But where in the ding-dong hell was I going to find Judy?

The cab stopped at the booth. I dialed my pad on an off chance. It was off, all right. No answer.

I decided that since the mess had begun at Funnyland, I would try that again. I paid off the cabbie and slogged my way along, heading for Stardust Heaven.

This establishment was likewise shut up tight. Boards were nailed across the pillars surrounding the open dance pavilion. Doubtless the eviction of Kewpie North & Co. had already been accomplished by Pop Toombs. One thread still dangled, however: was it Kewpie who had Judy?

I leaned against the pavilion pillars, sighing disconsolately. I surveyed the drifting crowds. Where the hell to go next?

The cops?

Who was kidding whom?

O.K., then ... what?

Perhaps I could pick up a lead at Judy's pitch. I ambled in that direction.

Half-way there, I passed one of those Fruit Ice wagons, its fluorescent lights leaking an unhealthy white color all over the asphalt. I had almost passed it when something registered. I waltzed on a few more feet, turned. I pretended to be engrossed in the garish painted canvas which advertised Farmingham's Fantastic & Formidable Freakshow, 17 Curiosities 17. But my real object was a man I'd seen before.

That Chinese type.

The item in the pince nez and homburg was paused at the Fruit Ice wagon, blandly munching the crushed frozen water in the paper cone, onto which somebody had squirted a lot of red juice.

Come, come, I thought. The days of the Oriental Menace are long past.

Yeah, but Wicks knew something about a spy apparatus. And he specifically mentioned Chinese. This guy had been floating around for at least a couple of days. Something went *tick* inside my skull as I reflected again on Miss Aloha Ross' vaguely Eurasian countenance. And Bark had told Goodpasture some pregnant facts about intelligence info filtering into Red China...

What could I lose except my dignity?

Pulling my porkpie down, I sidled over. The Chinese was crunching his colored ice. I slitted my eyes, jerked my head.

'Pssst!' I said, and walked off.

121

Seconds later, my heart going thump in my undersized ribcage, I turned back in a patch of shadow at the side of the street.

The Chinese was strolling toward me.

Lights flashed off his glasses. His smile was fixed and cherubic. 'Beg pardon, sir, but did you address me?'

'I certainly did,' I whispered. 'My name's Havoc.'

'Most honored to make your acquaintance,' he said with a neuter bob of his head. 'I am Mr. B. C. Chin, of San Francisco. I have been enjoying my holiday here very much. Although we have not met before that I know of, Mr. Havoc, courtesy compels me to inquire whether you would care to join me in a raspberry ice.' He wiggled his paper cone. 'Most delicious.'

'No, thanks. Listen ... I'm one of Aloha's boys.'

B. C. Chin munched his ice reflectively. 'I beg your pardon?'

'You heard me,' I hissed. 'Aloha, Aloha. I'm from Aloha.'

'From the Islands?' he said with a stupid blink.

Oh boy, I was laying a large bomb. Yet something in Chin's total lack of expression made me push on, only this time with more irritation and firmness.

'Chin, quit stalling. You know who I mean. Now pay attention, and if you don't want to play ball, say so. I'm supposed to report that we have the . . . ah . . . goods. The goods. Just tell me when we should make delivery, Chin. Tell me so I can go back and report to Aloha.'

The carousels went tinkle-tinkle. A rifle blasted in a shooting gallery. Mr. Chin's face remained carved out of a piece of low-grade souvenir ivory. The guy was probably going to holler copper and have me locked up for a nut.

Munch, munch. Mr. Chin devoured several more bites of his raspberry ice. His pince nez flashed light. Then he leaned forward.

'Here in America, Mr. Havoc, you operate in most unorthodox ways.'

My nerves knotted tight. Bullseye!

'It's the smartest way, Chin. Right out in the open. Has anybody bothered you? Or us? No, they just go about their business.'

And without so much as blinking, he said, 'And I am delighted that we shall soon conclude ours. Your report from Miss Ross is most welcome.' The joker actually bowed.

I tried to keep steady. 'Yeah . . . but when?'

'Shall we say a noon meeting, six days hence?'

'Six days! Chin, that's a pretty long time to wait for—'

'There is no choice, Mr. Havoc,' he cut in. The blandness was gone from his voice. His eyes were sharp and hard behind the glasses. 'Tonight is the last night I will be able to spend in this vicinity for several days. Another ... item of business ... compels me to leave for another part of the country. I will be unable to return until six days from now. It is then or not at all.' He added icily, 'The decision is in your hands, of course.'

I swallowed, 'Okay, Chin, okay. We want to do business. Six days. Noon. Here?'

'Shall we say in the little park beside the amusement device known as the—' (he dabbed at his lips in obvious distaste) '—Chutes-O-Fun? I will be waiting with the payment.'

All at once he became all business. He crushed up his empty cone of paper, stuck it in a trash bin and extended his hand. He gave my paw one brisk, no-nonsense pump, his bland little smile back in place. He tipped his homburg.

'Most honored to have made your acquaintance, Mr. Havoc. Please convey my regards to Miss Ross for an assignment well executed. Good evening.'

And off he traipsed, Fu Manchu in a business suit. He left me wondering just what the hell kind of a bag I was holding in my confused little hands. By the time I woke up, he had disappeared.

In a state of semi-daze, I headed for my original destination, Judy's pitch. I could not

124

believe any of what had just happened. My hunch had been one hundred percent correct, and all the things Bark told Goodpasture now made a ghastly kind of sense.

Yet my conversation with B. C. Chin smelled phony from beginning to end. Six days hence, noon, in the park beside the Chutes-O-Fun.

Havoc, thought I, you're being conned.

Yet I didn't know how or why. And somehow, I had the feeling that Chin was what he seemed to be—a very unfunny Oriental Menace bent on undermining the security of my own Homeland of Free Enterprise.

I was still trying to figure it out when I reached Judy's pitch. The Hareem of the Seven Veils was dark in front. Another fruitless effort, it seemed. Then I decided to check the back. I pussy-footed around there, and nearly whooped with joy when I noticed a gleam of weak light sifting under the canvas edge.

I darted forward, then skidded to a stop.

Nothing said it was Judy Swanson inside.

I sidled closer. I lifted the canvas cautiously and slipped inside. Hunched down in the darkness, I saw the plywood cubicle door half open. Clonk-clonk went a pair of shoes on the floorboards in there. The pacer came into view.

Not Judy Swanson at all. Lou Cyrus.

125

He passed the doorway again, frowning. The telephone rang. I stayed put, listening.

'Boss!' Cyrus exclaimed. 'I been waitin' for you. Sure I'm here. Listen ...' He lowered his voice. 'How is Judy? I mean ... is she okay? You haven't had to rough her up or anything like that?'

My fists knotted at my sides. I suppressed an urge to rush in there pell mell and bash Lou Cyrus in the face region. So Kewpie had Judy! He'd been the one who snatched her from my pad.

'That's good to hear, boss,' Cyrus was saying. 'I appreciate your taking it easy on her. She's a nice little broad, even though we have had our tiffs. What's that?'

Cyrus blinked at the AT&T equipment. 'Sure I've been doing what I'm supposed to be doing. Matter of fact, I've been hanging around this damn place for hours. I came straight here from that jerk Haddock's apartment, just like you told me. Listen, did you find anything when you searched her pad?'

Blink, blink, went Cyrus' eyelids. Pause, pause. His mouth turned down at the corners like a fish's.

'God, boss, I don't get it. Nothing at her place? Well, there's nothing here either. Boss, I don't see how she could know anything about what's going on. I've known Judy a couple of years, and she's never been mixed up in anything like spy stuff. Of course I'm sure! We were pretty close, if you know what I mean, until that wart Hammock came along.'

The foregoing was not as continuously delivered as all that, but was interspersed with many a grunt, whistle, eyebrow-lifting and so forth. During the pauses, I had a chance to dope out some of the more murky segments of the puzzle.

For example, I well remembered Kewpie's bugeyed assistant Fogel listening at the office door in Stardust Heaven when FitzHugh Goodpasture was spouting about spies, and papers worth a lot of money. Fogel doubtless put this news in front of Kewpie, who saw it as a gilt opportunity ... , and an opportunity he sorely needed, once his lease was busted and he was forced out to look for honest work.

Kewpie probably tumbled to the importance of what poor drunken Hopper T. Wicks had been muttering at the Stardust Heaven bar earlier. Since I had spirited Wicks away, and Kewpie had no way of knowing Inch had blasted him, Kewpie probably figured I could be found, with the Valuable Mr. Wicks, at my pad. At least he had no doubt begun looking there, after finding my address in the all-too-public phone directory.

Instead of me, he had found Judy ... and

the attaché case.

Whose contents—it was the biggest, unfunniest joke of all—now appeared to be worthless.

Kewpie's latest frantic searchings of Judy's apartment and the pitch here indicated to me that he was as confused over the junk in the case as I was. That, however, helped Judy not one whit.

'Where do you want me to meet you, Kewpie? Where are you holed up?' (Pause, pause.) 'Boss, you're kidding! The Brummel Place? That old joint in the woods? The one with the white siding and green roof? My God, boss! That's on the property those sojers are going to use for their war games tomorrow. Didn't you read about it in the papers?'

Another long interval.

'But it's dangerous! We might get shelled! We might get—yes, boss.' Cyrus was suddenly meek. He held the receiver, which I could hear rattling and crackling, away from his ear. By profanity, Kewpie was convincing his minion that the Brummel Place was ideal as a temporary hideout.

'Yes, boss. Sure, boss. I understand, boss. Listen, are you calling from the Brummel Place now? Oh, you're not. O.K., how soon shall I meet you? Sure, I can come right away. See you. And boss. Thanks for taking it easy on Judy, huh?'

Wiping his forehead and shaking his head, Lou Cyrus hung up.

He zipped up his windbreaker, snapped out the light. I froze in the darkness as he passed within an ace of where I was crouched.

The tent flap rustled. Lou Cyrus' footsteps clacked on the asphalt outside. I counted, 'One, America, two, America,' up to ten, and then ducked after him.

He was heading down the narrow passageway between the tents, moving fast, off to my left. I went in pursuit.

Three steps was the extent of my journey.

The first warning was the aroma of cloves drifting out of the dark. Gnarled hands came reaching, and I let out a gargle as they closed around my windpipe.

'Leggo!' I yelled. It came out a squeak. Towering up, big Inch was choking the hell out of me.

He lifted me off the pavement. He dangled me in mid-air. It hurt. Purple spots danced around inside my head.

Desperately I tried to kick his shinbones. The kick never connected. Something unpleasantly hard ground into the small of my small back.

'Put him down, Inch. The gun will do it much more efficiently if he struggles.'

Inch did not neglect the opportunity to slam me down so violently that my teeth ached. While I was recovering, Miss Aloha

Ross stepped around in front of me. She wore no makeup. Instead of her red hostess outfit, she had on a man's oyster-colored raincoat with the collar turned up and the belt snugged tight. A scarf was tied around her hair. In her pretty little gloved right fist gleamed a nasty snub-muzzle automatic.

'Pardon me for not being able to figure out how you turned up here,' I wheezed.

Aloha shrugged. 'The news traveled rather fast about the escape of a small civilian fitting your description from Fort Parnell, dear man. After all, it's hard to keep word of a semi-riot from the news media. Actually, I imagined you would know better than to revisit the proverbial scene of the crime.' She tickled me under the chin with the muzzle, taking pains to dig around in my flesh with the sharp sight. 'However, it's clear that you didn't. So perhaps we can finish our chat.'

Her smile went away. She was Grade A Nasty when she spat, 'We will finish our chat, dear man, or I will have Inch finish you. Permanently.'

'The only conversation I intend to have with you, cookie, is—'

Blappo! Inch gave it to me in the back of the neck with his double fist.

I reeled forward, munched some asphalt, and before I could say, 'Poor Judy!', the ugly hauled me up, and he and Aloha marched me along the alley between the tents.

130

Straight toward what looked like the end of the road.

CHAPTER ELEVEN

Presently we were marching down one of the main streets of Funnyland. Aloha linked her arm with mine and proceeded to giggle and wiggle as we marched along, in a perfect imitation of a dolly out to see the sights with a couple of friends.

Inch stayed equally close on the other side, Aloha's cannon in the pocket of his jacket. Aloha had already bent toward my ear with an ersatz sweet-nothings smile on her map as she whispered:

'If you so much as stumble, dear little man, Inch will fire, and we'll take our chances on getting away.'

Soon we reached the main parking lot. I was propelled into the right-hand front seat of the same heap in which Inch had motored me to the Grove the first time. The pug climbed under the wheel. Aloha took the cannon in back. Puffing a smokey with one hand and holding the rod in the other, she gave me a smirk.

'Really, Havoc, that was a frightful blunder.'

'Which one? I've made so many.'

'I'm referring to your encounter with B. C. Chin.'

I played dumb. 'B. C. who?'

Aloha wigwagged her filtertip deprecatingly. 'Oh, come now, dear. Obviously you know B. C. Chin. You had a conversation with him in the park earlier this evening. You see, dear man,' she added with the saccharin dripping in her tone, 'I had talked to him just about half an hour before you.'

That was a bomb. 'You ... talked to ... ?'

Aloha leaned over and gave my chin a nasty pinch. 'Yes, dear. Just a few moments before you blundered onto him, we had met at a certain place in Funnyland. And after your conversation, he immediately rushed to a phone booth and called my number.'

All I could say was, 'Why?'

'To learn, of course, who you were. You were passing yourself off as some sort of assistant of mine. Trying to make arrangements for delivery of certain ... merchandise ... when in fact Mr. Chin and I, at our meeting, had already agreed that the transfer of the ... package ... would take place at 6 p.m. tomorrow evening in the park, when the customary Saturday crowds will make such a transfer that much more convenient.'

'The lousy, stinking fortune cookie!' I muttered. 'He suckered me!'

Aloha was enjoying it no end. 'Yes, he did. He pretended to agree to a fictitious rendezvous next week, so that he could get away and learn, if possible, who you were.'

'I thought it seemed too damn easy. That'll teach me to bluff.'

'Your little attempts to play detective put me in an embarrassing position,' Aloha continued. 'Actually, B. C. Chin really did not know whether you were or were not working for me. To protect my—shall we say—image of efficiency, and to prevent Mr. Chin from thinking that I had bungled in any way, I was forced to lie to him. I must protect my income, you know. And my income depends on payments received from gentlemen like Chin. So I admitted, with suitable apologies, that you were indeed one of my men. And that you had the signals fouled up.'

As I reached in my pocket for a butt, Inch made a threatening lurch in my direction. Aloha waved him back. The match I lit put ugly little patches of orange light on her face, showing me just how tough and vicious she really was, under her veneer of sexy-dolly paint.

'It confuses me, Aloha.'

'What does, dear?'

'Your telling Chin I was one of your boys. How could you get away with that?'

'By theorizing that you'd undoubtedly

contacted him before you were aware that I had changed my mind. I pretended that I had indeed planned to transfer the merchandise next week. But had decided at the last moment that a delivery tomorrow would be safer. Actually, B. C. Chin was delighted. He looked on my change of heart as double protection. If, for some unforeseen reason, the package could not be transferred to him tomorrow, Saturday, then the rendezvous next week—in six days, wasn't it?—would serve the same purpose. And now ...' She wigwagged the cannon slightly. The inside of the car was a tight, smoke-choked, stuffy little world all of its own, and the glimmering bulbs in Funnyland might as well have been lighthouses on Mars. '... shall we dispense with conversation except on topics of importance? Where is the case?'

Inch laid his paw on my arm and constricted his fingers. He smiled like a grave-robber. 'Either we get it while you're in one piece, midget, or we get it while you're in little pieces. One way or another, we're gonna get it.'

I pried Inch's pinkies loose, turned around in the seat, trying to stall the dolly:

'You want the case so you can sell the contents of Mr. Chin, huh?'

'That is correct,' said Aloha sweetly.

'In other words, you're a spy.'

'Havoc, I warn you. Further delays will

134

only—'

'For God's sakes, you've got me cold!' I broke in. 'At least let me go out with some of the pieces in place, huh?'

Aloha gnawed her luscious underlip, glanced at her wristwatch. Since she showed signs of hesitating, I plunged ahead:

'How come, for instance, you happened to tumble to Edson being a fed?'

You'd have thought I asked a Ph.D. how to spell cat. 'Oh, that's too simple, darling. Soon after joining the mob controlled by that dull-witted Kewpie North, Edson realized the mob couldn't be handling military secrets, because their combined mentalities were too low for anything except petty extortion. So Edson began searching for another lead. One night he visited The Bamboo Grove. Inch was tending bar. Inch inquired whether Edson was a salesman, since he'd never seen him before. And what did Mr. Edson reply, Inch?'

'He said, nah, he wasn't no salesman, he worked around Funnyland. Then he told me all about his fight with that meat-brain Fogel.'

'So?' I said.

'So,' Aloha continued, 'Edson was no doubt passing out all this information gratis, as part of his mobster cover. Unfortunately, that same evening, Edson noticed me talking with Hopper Wicks at the bar. We were . . .

behaving in a rather intimate way.' She made a face. 'Wicks was a disgusting boob, but I had no choice. At the time, however, I had no way of knowing that Edson had seen Hopper Wicks earlier. That same day, in fact.'

I was confused about how she knew all this, but let it ride, saying, 'Where?'

'Near Fort Parnell. Edson made regular trips to watch the perimeter of the Fort. He spied Wicks driving out in his car after making a sales call. So, in an instant, there at the Grove bar, Edson had part of his answer ... including why Inch here was curious about whether he was a salesman. It was really a bit of bad luck that Edson showed up when Wicks was present too. I noticed Edson watching us, and I particularly noticed his long jaw. But I really had no suspicions about him until later. I was too busy with Hopper.'

'Setting him up for murder.' I shook my head. 'A swell bunch of patriots.'

'Wave the flag all you wish, dear,' Aloha cooed nastily. 'It's not my flag.'

'That's for damn sure.'

'Do you want to hear more?' she snapped. 'If so, be quiet.'

'O.K., keep talking.'

'Inch reported later that Edson had been paying particular attention to Hopper Wicks and me. So I sent Inch to follow Edson. Inch surprised him at the apartment near Funnyland where he was living. He

136

overpowered Edson and ... disposed of him. Quite necessary, I'm afraid. But Inch, the dear boy, was clever enough to drop him on the doorstep of Kewpie North, to make it look like a gang killing. Then Inch returned with the report he had discovered Edson writing in his quarters. Frankly, I was annoyed with Inch for being so precipitous with his pistol until I read that report. I read it and burned it. It was quite damaging. From that report, incidentally, I learned most of what I've just told you about the inquisitive Mr. Edson's thought processes in discovering what I was doing. One line in particular made me glad he was dead. It ran something like, "... *must put a tracer on her. Have HQ see whether they can check her real identity.*"'

Another callous shrug, as if Edson's execution represented merely one more lead-filled milk bottle to be knocked off its perch in a carny game. 'Edson's noise about having quarrelled with Fogel was the perfect excuse for assigning guilt to Kewpie North's group. So there you have the story, dear little man. Are you satisfied?'

I ground the butt out in the dash tray. 'Not quite. Who are you? I mean for real?'

'Oh, come now. That's not necessary.'

'Maybe not. But don't I have the right to know who's creaming me? That is,' I added, with my cowardice working overtime, 'if you

137

are not going to cream me.'

'How clever of you! How did you guess? Very well, Havoc. My name is not Ross. It's Anastasia Ree. I was born in Singapore. My parents were Eurasian. I've been—shall we say—a free-lance agent for some eight years.'

'And partial to the line of crud peddled by Peking?'

'Call it what you will,' she said frigidly, 'it represents the wave of the future. Actually my allegiance is one part idealism and one part vested interest. They pay well. They were paying particularly well for my having made Hopper Wicks my latest conquest. Poor Hopper, it turned out, also noticed Edson watching us that night at the bar. He too was struck by that peculiar long jaw of Mr. Edson's. Next day, he saw that identical jaw spread on the front pages of the morning papers, together with an account of how Edson had been found slain.'

The same pic had been spread out in Kewpie North's office. I nodded. 'Yeah, keep going.'

'I had been stringing poor Hopper along by making him believe I was in love with him. As soon as Edson was killed, though, Wicks grew suspicious. He rushed to the Grove to "confront" me. At that early morning hour I was unprepared for visitors. He discovered me writing a report about peanut butter, toothpaste and photographic film. Hopper realized that he himself, unwittingly, had provided me with some of the information about the peanut butter. He was an awful blabber, especially when he was drinking. Well, he grew quarrelsome, hit Inch over the head with his sample case of peanut butter jars, snatched the report and ran.'

At last I was making nutty sense of it. 'Straight to the bar at Stardust Heaven, to drown his woes in sauce. And I already know how he got cooled.'

'Then you're completely up to date. Now, I want that attaché case with no further delay. It's worth a minimum of eighty-five thousand U.S. dollars, to be paid to me by Mr. Chin's government.'

The conviction that she was totally cuckoo still bothered me. Peanut butter? Toothpaste? Madness! But the desperation of the moment, and my urge for green, made me play along.

'Did you sell the first package of information to B. C. Chin too, doll?'

'Which package?' she returned without hesitation.

'Come off it! The one the U.S. spy boys already turned up in Hong Kong.'

'You do acquire the most unusual bits of information,' she said, shaking her head. 'Yes, I conducted that transaction.'

'Then, lady,' I said, 'you are nuts.'

Inch manhandled my cartilage in the vicinity of my shoulder. 'Watch it, creep.'

'This is the biggest con I've ever seen!' I yelled. 'Selling facts about peanut butter to the Chinese for eighty-five grand! Who's diddling whom?'

'Obviously, Havoc,' said Aloha icily, 'you know nothing about intelligence.'

'I know you've lost yours somewhere along the line.'

That got her goat. She waved the cannon at my schnozz, her voice edged with irritation. 'Are you accusing me of not knowing my trade, Havoc? That proves what a fool you are! Just how would you go about learning the strength and organization of the troops at Fort Parnell? Would you feed the soldiers doped drinks? That's cheap, obvious, dangerous, and out of date. I worked hard, Havoc, nine long months, to land the job as hostess and manager of The Bamboo Grove. I didn't want the job because soldiers from the Fort dropped in there. That approach went out with silent pictures. Whether you realize it or not, the bar at the Grove is one of the favorite stopping places of certain gentlemen who work in the area. Salesmen.'

Feeling slightly thick, I said, 'And?'

'And, rather than doing what you, an obvious victim of too many cheap novels and television plays, think an espionage agent would do—blackjack a soldier after he was drugged, or some other ridiculous thing—I worked carefully on a different tack. I took a

140

full twelve months assembling that first package of information which went to Hong Kong. And I did it by conducting three separate and discreet affairs with three very carefully set up salesmen. And I did exactly the same thing for this second, current package. First there was Gower, the toothpaste salesman. Then Ralph, the snapshot film salesman. Then Hopper, the—'

'I can't stand this!' I cried. 'Peanut butter is peanut butter!'

'Not to an expert.'

'What?'

'Peanut butter is the raw material of intelligence.'

'Boloney! I've never heard of anything so crazy.'

With cool contempt, she shrugged. 'Obviously ... too many cheap films. They try to suggest that the trade of intelligence is the one time transfer of the super-secret plans for The Great Death Ray. Nonsense! At least it's nonsense 99 percent of the time. Intelligence, for your information, is a whole host of rather dull little pieces which fit together into one large mosaic.'

She raised her hand and ticked off her fingernails with the muzzle of the cannon. 'Things like noting ship sailings. Gathering and interpreting clippings from technical journals. And, in the case of Fort Parnell, putting together a report on the sales volume of selected articles at the Fort PX and commissary. You see, Havoc, by knowing the per capita consumption of peanut butter in the U.S., Havoc, an intelligence professional can extrapolate from the Fort sales figures and arrive at almost the exact number of men who are consuming the horrid stuff. With figures on film sales and toothpaste added, it becomes a triple, nearly foolproof index of the strength of the base.'

I may have felt duller at other times, but I couldn't remember when. 'My God,' I said. 'It's the most unlikely thing I have ever heard. Which means it's probably true.'

'Of course it is.' She sniffed. 'You insult me by suggesting otherwise.' Then her brows hooked together. Once more she let me see the operating end of the cannon. 'I'm afraid my patience is wearing a trifle thin. You have gotten all the explanation from me which you are going to get. Where is the attaché case containing my report?'

Inch hitched toward me on the front seat, displaying his dentalware. 'Just say you don't know, midget. Just say that and I can go to work finding out.'

My belly was icy, but my mind was jumping all over. 'But I do know.'

Aloha recoiled. 'What did you say?'

'I said, of course I know where the attaché case is. I'll get it for you.'

'We'll get it,' she purred.

'Oh no we won't!' I yelled. 'Oh no, we won't get a double-damned thing, baby!'

Despite the horrific aspects of my predicament—a predicament which could certainly get no worse, no matter what happened—the tantalizing smell of green bills was running high. Perhaps it was because I was half asleep by now, it being around two in the morning, and the last attractions at Funnyland, the eating joints with late-closing licenses, were shutting finally down. While our little interview had been going on, cars had been departing from the lot right and left, but of course everybody was in such a damned hurry to get home to the Beautyrest, they never bothered with a second glance at the three folks having a friendly chat in Aloha's heap.

'I fail to understand your sudden confidence,' Aloha said. 'You are in no position—'

'Beg pardon, honey, but I'm in the perfect position.' I was conning for all I was worth. 'It boils down to this. Either you play my way or you don't play at all.'

'The gall!' Aloha gasped. 'You can't get away from us, Havoc.'

I nodded. 'Not unless you let me go.'

'Let you go! Of all the absurd—!'

'Now wait a second! Even if you do let me waltz out of this buggy, don't you think I know you would catch up to me and fry me if

143

I crossed you? Which is exactly why, Miss Ross, you are going to let me out. Because if you don't—' (I wagged my index finger as hard as she'd waved the rod's muzzle a while back) '—you can have your bruiser pulverize me to a fare-thee-well, and you won't learn a thing. Not one blessed thing. Not where the attaché case is—nothing! I'll travel to the mortuary with my mouth shut tight, I promise you.'

Tension, as they say in those pain-reliever commercials, mounted up.

Aloha hesitated. She peered at me closely. Inch strained to begin battering. I tried to keep a cocky look on my puss as the seconds ticked away.

At last, looking slightly desperate, Aloha spoke.

'Twelve hours, dear little man. Twelve hours ...' She glanced at her watch. 'That would make it approximately two o'clock, Saturday afternoon. You meet me outside Stardust Heaven with that attaché case or I swear to God we'll find you. We'll find you and kill you.'

'I know,' I said. 'And that's why I'll be there.'

I reached for the car door handle. Inch jerked up his fists.

'Let him go!' Aloha ordered. Inch grumbled. I bounced out of the car. Her voice whispered in the night air.

144

'Two o'clock tomorrow morning. Or you're a dead man, Johnny Havoc.'

A moment later, Inch gunned the bus out of the lot. I was all by myself, my mental companion being the thought that, unless I could figure some way to keep from giving her the case while avoiding getting shot, four hours after I turned the case over to her, she would rendezvous with Mr. B. C. Chin and send the info away on the Orient Express.

Well, I was alive, though. And temporarily free.

It was scant consolation.

Especially since I didn't even have the attaché case to begin with.

Benedict Havoc, that was me.

Or Havoc the Corpse.

Either way, it stacked up as a stinking choice.

CHAPTER TWELVE

The stars were out. The sky was clear. For a few seconds, I felt immensely sorry for yours truly, all by his lonesome out there in the middle of the night.

I suppressed a yawn. Then along came one I couldn't suppress. After so many hours of bumps and lumps, weariness finally settled over my undersized person.

145

Since Judy had taken my heap, I had no transportation to a motel. I would have to make do. Of the three heaps left me in the lot, one was open. In its back seat I came upon a veritable treasure of nourishment, half of a faintly petrified Hershey bar.

I sat in the car munching the goody and recalling that Lou Cyrus had made arrangements to rendezvous with Kewpie North & Mob at some joint called The Brummel Place off in the woods. At that rendezvous I might find both the attaché case upon which my skin depended, and Judy Swanson. Ergo, it was The Brummel Place for me. I didn't know how to locate it. But there couldn't be too many dumps sitting around amid the trees which sported white siding and a green roof.

But first, the inner man, and the outer one, too, had to rest.

I started trudging. Soon I was knee deep in weeds and ploughing wearily toward a thick stand of trees all black and gloomy ahead. The lights of Funnyland, save for a few faint service bulbs, had been extinguished. It was lonely as hell out there in the country.

My mind was beginning to boggle from tiredness. As I reached the edge of the trees, I heard a snapping and crackling behind me. I imagined I was imagining it. I stumbled into a tree trunk.

'Oh, pardon me,' I said vaguely. The

146

crackling was repeated. I stopped.

I sidled around the tree and peered back toward the open field. A massive set of shoulders and a head ducked out of sight.

Noisily I proceeded a few more yards through the trees.

Crackle-snap, rustle-rattle.

I turned back again. The shadowy bulk in the field once more dropped down. I leaned against some bark and sighed.

Well, I might have guessed Miss Aloha wouldn't simply let me vanish. She had probably told Inch to get out of the car after she pulled away from the lot, and now the big ox was tagging along behind, with as much finesse as a calliope playing at the public library.

Once more I tried the move-and-stop game.

Once more he advanced and stopped, right with me.

His latest maneuver brought him to the edge of the woods. Starlight winked on unpleasant blue gun metal. I preceeded a distance further, found a relatively dry bed of leaves under a tree, and settled down. I pulled my porkpie over my face and listened.

A similar rustling stopped suddenly. Inch had halted too.

A few more minutes of alertness, intermixed with yawns, indicated that Inch's object must be to keep me in sight. For as I stayed put, so did he. I turned up my coat

147

collar and went to sleep.

★   ★   ★

Cherry yellow sunlight peeked under the brim of my porkpie some hours later.

I yawned, pushed the hat back. A nuthatch sitting on a twig a few inches from my outstretched foot took off in a ruffle of feathers.

The air in the woods smelled of dew and early morning. The slant of the sun, plus the faint mist curling through the trees, indicated it was just past sunrise. So did my watch, which was in the last stages of running down.

I wound it, wished I had another Hershey bar, got up, peered through the trees.

No sign of Inch. But I was sure he was there.

I thought a while. I decided I had better ditch him. I had no notions of how to do it. I decided next to walk a bit and wait until my brain de-fogged.

I set off into the woods. Sure enough, the *carrumph* of his brogans came drifting through the thinning mist, which the sun was slowly sizzling off.

'Okay, Havoc,' I said half-aloud. 'What happens now? Track shoes you ain't got.'

No one answered except the nuthatches in the treetops. I started jogtrotting. Inch kept pace.

148

A little clearing opened up ahead. I figured I would try one of the tactics of one of the companions of my misspent youth, The Ape Man, himself. I picked out a likely, thick-leafed tree, jumped, caught a lower branch and managed to hook my legs up and over.

I climbed to a fork and hunched down, watching out below. Pretty soon Inch came dogging it along through the flora, his cannon in his mitt. I held my breath.

'Now where in the hell is he?' Inch was muttering.

That, as you might guess, was when the slightly rotted branch upon which my left foot was braced, decided to give up the ghost as well as its attachment to the tree.

I heard a sickly scr-runch. Suddenly there was nothing below my left loafer but air. I hollered, 'Help!' without thinking and fell.

Conk! The limb hit Inch.

Conk! I followed it immediately.

Flattened, Inch let out a yowl. 'Dirty, sneaky little bas—'

'Have some leaves, punchy!' I cried, jamming a branch down on the back of his pate with my shoe. I took off.

More curses. Then, a flat, loud plopping. A large hunk of bark on a tree which I was pelting past disappeared as the bullet dug a channel.

My heart began to go faster than my legs.

149

Inch was up, I saw, leaves and twigs still stuck in his garments, and his face set into nasty lines. I jumped bushes, bungled into a creek, went splashing across with cuffs afloat, panted up the other side. I didn't see the sneaky, overgrown root upon which my shoe caught suddenly.

'Yow!' The landscape went tilt.

Earth met my nose. My chest hurt. I tried to push up with my palms, just as Inch came noisily across the creek with a vicious grin on his face and his pistola aimed.

'So!' he said, giving me a belt in the backside. 'So, you little bastard, just like Miss Ross thought—you were doing the bug-out bit. You never did figure we'd ... figure we'd ... figure we'd...'

I wanted to suggest he fix his needle. He kept saying that. Something was troubling him. Something behind me which, because of my undignified position, I was unable to see.

Curious, I wrenched my cranium around. I goggled.

The animated furpiece had apparently been roused by the shot. The furpiece walked on all fours out from some bosky den and was now confronting us with its wet black nose twitching and its brown fur quivering and its small eyes gleaming with what I assumed was an urge to do violence to our persons. Inch's cannon-hand shook.

'A b—b—bear. My God, look at the

b—b—bear.'

The furpiece scratched its long, unpleasant front claws in the earth, as if honing them. Then the creature started forward. Inch snatched up a rock.

'You damn fool!' I howled. 'Don't throw that! You'll get it more sore than it already—'

Whizzo! The stone bopped the bear on the pate.

The creature reared up on its hind legs, went, 'Gnarrrh! Gnarrh! Gnarrh!' whilst pawing the air. Then it dropped down fast and began to pad forward, snarling and baring its molars.

As I got to my feet, I espied a bunch of berries hanging from a cluster-heavy bush. 'Distract it, distract it!' I hissed to Inch. But the big hooligan was hunting around for another rock.

I grabbed the bunch of berries and tossed it through the air. 'Nice bear, nice bear.'

With one claw-heavy paw, the monster batted the berries away. *'Gnarrrh!'*

Never taking my eyes off the thing, I started to back up. I bumped against Inch. 'Get moving!' I hissed. He chuckled. Then he struck me in the small of the back with the flat of his free hand.

Arms pumping, I flew straight at the furpiece's hungry chops.

'Oh, you sneaky son of a bitch!' I hollered, off-balance and tumbling straight toward

151

those gleaming molars. I fell flat on the sod. The bear went chomp, just missing me. He was moving fast. By jamming my legs together and covering my head with my arms, I pulled the old Saturday serial bit, where the dauntless hero lies on the railroad tracks while the wheels clip by him on either side, and the bottom of the boxcar narrowly shaves the top of his head.

The bear charged over me, skidded to a halt. By that time I was up and turning fast.

'He's the one who's been eating your porridge, get him!' I cried with some hysteria as I kicked the bear in his hind quarters. This, plus the sight of Inch quivering and shivering directly ahead of him, must have convinced the furpiece that Inch would make the better meal.

The bear took off for him like an express.

'Yiiiiii!' Inch turned tail.

The last I saw of him, he was hoofing it through the forest primeval as fast as he could go, too scared to stop and try his cannon. The furpiece was right on his heels. I commenced to get out of that neighborhood as fast as possible.

After about a half an hour of tramping, my heartbeat began to slow down again. I reached the edge of this patch of woods. I peered out.

More woods ahead. To reach them, I had to cross another open field. I hadn't gone more than half way when I heard a motor.

The grass was high. A little knoll rose on my left. Behind that, the motor noise grew louder. I did the swan act into the undergrowth, lay there breathing hard as the motor ground closer, passed, then began to recede. When the vehicle drove out from behind the cover of the knoll, I saw what it was—a U.S. Army jeep loaded with tough apples in camouflage togs, paratroop boots and green berets.

Another jeep went roaring down the dirt road after it, then a third. Silence. A bird chirruped.

'If you had any sense,' I said to the flying fowl, 'you would get the hell out of this vicinity,' But like me, it didn't have any sense.

I pressed on, even though I had just recalled that this was the day on which the war games sponsored by Fort Percy Parnell were to be conducted on this same terrain.

After making sure no more vehicles were about, I trotted toward the woods ahead, reached their welcome cover and thanked my stars I had not been spotted.

Trying to keep my bearings by the sun, I ankled on through the conglomeration of forestry for about five minutes before sighting a white glimmer up ahead. I began to move forward more cautiously.

Tree trunk by tree trunk, I approached.

153

Soon I had a pretty good view of the place. It was a dilapidated old dump whose peeled siding displayed areas of white paint. Around several large holes in the roof, green shingles remained. The Brummel Place, without a doubt.

It had a wide front porch, third-story dormers, and a flattened picket fence around it. Weeds choked the yard. A dirt road running through the trees approached from the left and disappeared on the right. The property was located behind that road.

A couple of finches flew around the chimney. Otherwise the place looked deserted. From the main road, if you could call it that, a dirt driveway circled around back outside the picket fence.

Hell! I'd risked life, limb and sanity to get here, and nothing seemed to be happening. Of course most of the windows were shuttered and those that weren't had a covering of dirt and cobwebs. I decided to check the rear before jumping to any more conclusions.

I circled wide to the right, through the trees, crossed the dirt road and worked my way up from behind. As I drew near, I lamped a sedan parked behind the joint, out of sight from the main road. The sedan's paint gleamed dully in the sun, covered by a layer of dust. A late model. But abandoned . . . ?

I needed a closer look.

I stood up, swallowed hard, emerged from the trees and began to pad cautiously toward the sagging back porch. I approached the sedan, passed it, and heard a faint buzzing. I glanced around, hunting for bees.

I didn't see any bees.

I put my foot on the bottom riser of the rickety back steps, tested my weight and cringed when the boards squeaked.

A person sat up in the rear seat of the sedan.

The bee-buzz had been snoring.

The person lamped me. I lamped him. I recognized the gentleman known as Rix.

'Hold it, hold it!' Rix croaked, out of the auto and shoving his cannon in my ribcage before I could so much as move. He turned toward the house, bawled, 'Hey! Hey, fellas! Hey, come out here! Look what I found.'

Then he gave me a nasty grimace. 'Lucky I woke up when I did, huh? Otherwise Kewpie'd of give me hell. I was supposed to be on watch.'

The commandos smacked open the back door and came pouring onto the rickety porch, pushing, shoving, unlimbering their heaters.

Chief among them was my nemesis, Mr. Kewpie North.

CHAPTER THIRTEEN

Upon seeing me, Mr. Kewpie North practically bit the plastic tip of his cigar in half.

'The wart! The little creep! What the hell is he doing nosing around here, Rix?'

Poor Rix look befogged. 'Don't get sore at me, chief. I caught him, dint I?'

'Yeah, guess you did.'

Kewpie darted me a particularly malevolent glance, smoothed down his tonicked hair with one hand, and jerked the other, including thumb, at the squeaky screen door.

'Inside, Haddock. Maybe you can help us with that crappola in the bag. In fact, you better if you don't want to end up marmalade. Oh, Fogel! I got somebody out here for you to handle.'

Preceded by his bulging eyes, Fogel appeared in the screened opening. Those orbs stood out another half inch at least when they lit upon me. Fogel zipped outside, cracking his knuckles.

'Why, look who's here! The weisenheimer. He doesn't look very wise now, does he?' Fogel held the screen open. 'Care to step inside, buddy boy?'

I gave a weary shrug. 'Who's got a choice?'

156

'My,' said Fogel, 'you get smarter every second.'

Just as I was passing into the dim interior of an old kitchen that reeked of scouring cleanser and linoleum, Fogel hauled off and cracked me in the back of the neck. This caused the group of hoods to chortle merrily. I bounced off the floor, staggered up groggy and mad, and was about ready to turn and start swinging despite the odds when somebody screeched my name.

At the end of a hallway, sun motes danced dustily in a parlor. There were a couple of people in there. One wore a striped sport shirt and a suspicious expression. The other was small, neatly packaged, pale, and—

'Judy! My God, are you all right?'

Before they could lay a hand on me, I hotfooted down the hall into the parlor. But the sport shirt, which was filled by Lou Cyrus, barred my way.

'Of course she's all right. I look out for my girl, don't you worry.'

Over his shoulder, poor Judy made a face.

Cyrus, both baffled and amused, asked, 'Hey, boss, where'd you come across peewee here?'

Kewpie shouldered past, managing to give me a shove so that my face smashed into the doorjamb. 'We found him nosing around outside. Haddock, you go in there and siddown.' He shoved. I collapsed into a needlepoint rocker that gave off a squeak and sent up a cloud of dust which nearly choked me. Judy looked at me with a sorrowful expression. She seemed tired, bedraggled, but unhurt.

Kewpie applied a chrome lighter to his weed. 'Lou baby, shall we continue our discussion of what is going to happen to your female playmate? It's a drag, taking care of her. Let's settle it one way or the other.'

'What's to settle?' Cyrus asked. 'She doesn't know anything.'

'Doesn't know anything my pratt! She had that, didn't she?'

That, which I had not spotted before, was the black attaché case with silver trim. It reposed on an old claw-legged table covered with dust. I struggled to control my rapid breathing. The peanut butter dossier! Worth eighty-five thousand clams, and within snatching distance.

And I couldn't snatch it.

I pretended disinterest when I noticed Fogel studying me. I let my gaze rove around the parlor. Sheets had been jerked off the furniture. The lace curtains were falling into yellow tatters. Everything was dusty, and there were all sorts of knicknacks piled here and there: a stuffed moose head, a porcelain chamber pot, two busted coat trees, a big leather-bound trunk, some yellowed 1920 magazines, and other oddments. The parlor was like a junkshop, and the way things were going, Judy and I might end up as two more relics among the junk.

'I say,' Kewpie emphasized using his weed, 'she helped him, she had the case, she was in cahoots with him, so we ought to chill her.'

Judy blanched. They weren't kidding. But Cyrus shook his head. 'Listen, Kewpie, she may be no damn good, but she's my girl. Or she was, until that fast-talking little mother came along. I don't want anything to happen to her. I . . .' Cyrus lowered his voice. 'Look, can't we talk about this in private?'

Kewpie debated mentally. 'Fogel! Throw those two in the next room for a while.'

Thus we were locked in with a big old fourposter.

Judy made commiserating sounds. Her big blue eyes had begun to fill with tears. I collected myself, shushed her with a finger to the lips, and hustled to the one and only window.

'Rats!'

I let the shade fall back into place. A thug with a cannon lounged on the porch just outside. In the parlor, the voices had dropped to indecipherable murmurs. Judy came close.

'Are you all right, Johnny?'

'Peachy. But how about you, hon? Have they hurt you?'

'No, but I've been awfully frightened,' she admitted. Suddenly her delicious arms went

159

around my neck. She pressed close, her five-foot size just about matching my own inch-higher stature. She snuggled against me. 'Lou Cyrus still thinks I'm his girl. You heard him. After what's happened, I'd sooner kiss a lizard. But ... because I was kind of scared, I let Lou go on thinking what he wanted to think.'

'Don't worry, that's O.K.'

'Johnny?'

'What?'

'Will we ... get out of this?'

Even though the situation to me looked totally hopeless, I felt it was my responsibility to be Morale Leader for the group. 'Sure. I'll think of something. In the meantime, I'm glad to see you. And I'm not a lizard. At least I don't think so.'

Softly she said, 'I don't think so either, Johnny.'

And gave me a smooch.

It really was meant to be a morale booster for both of us, I guess. But what with one thing and another, my hormones started doing nip-ups. She squeezed hard and gave a few wriggles against my person with her delectable just-the-right-size assets. I was still bussing her when I heard a door go bang.

'Guess what, Judy! I fixed it so Kewpie promised he wouldn't—hey! What the hell!'

Rapidly I disengaged. 'Uh ... we were just renewing acquaintances.'

160

Lou Cyrus colored. 'Judy, what is this? I mean, what is this?'

Now Judy had her temper up. 'What do you think it is, you crooked, conceited oaf?'

'You ... you and this wart ... ?'

'Judy,' I said, 'let's not be too hasty. Mr. Cyrus has a lot to recommend him.'

She didn't get the idea of humoring him. Temper and tension got in the way. Several of the hoods peered in from the parlor, sniggering. Judy marched up to Cyrus.

'Like I told Johnny a minute ago, I'd sooner kiss a lizard than you, Lou Cyrus. If you think I'd ever take up with you again, you're just plain cockeyed!'

All sorts of emotions flashed across Cyrus' map then. Over his shoulder he yelled, 'Hey, Kewpie! Forget what I said about this lousy little broad. Throw her to the dogs along with peewee.' Kewpie laughed, said something about knowing Lou would see it his way. Lou doubled his fists. 'But first, I'm going to beat hell out of this little runt.'

Judy screamed. Cyrus swung. I ducked. Cyrus' fist smashed the bedpost.

The blow was enough. One of the fourposter's legs collapsed. The mattress split in several places. Lou Cyrus was covered from head to foot with a drifing, swirling cloud of duck feathers.

Spitting and batting at them, he shambled toward me again. Fortunately, Kewpie and

161

Rix bounded into the room.

'Cool it, Lou!' Kewpie said. 'I said cool it!' Kewpie grabbed him, backhanded him three times.

Cyrus' eyes appeared to rotate, each in the opposite direction. Kewpie turned him around, shoved him toward the parlor, barked, 'I got better things to do with the runt than let you mess him up. Now you haul it out on that front porch damn quick and keep your eyes peeled for any sojers that may be pussyfooting around. Rix, go with him. See that he stays put.'

Torn between jealousy and duty, Cyrus chose the latter, though not before yelling over his shoulder, 'O.K., but I don't give a damn what you do with that cheating little broad now.'

'Judy,' I said, 'I'm sorry. I didn't mean to get you in trouble.'

'Very touching, very touching,' opined Kewpie, kicking me in the kiester. 'Get out there in the parlor where we can have a little confab, midget.'

They hauled Judy along too. They plunked me down in the rocker. Fogel stood behind the chair, cracking his knuckles now and then. Kewpie assumed an oratorical pose in the middle of the threadbare carpet.

'Let me put it to you plain, midget. I know there's hot stuff in that case. But it's all a lot of gibberish as far as I'm concerned. Peanut

162

butter? Film? Toothpaste? Who needs it?' Then he cackled. 'Somebody, Haddock! Somebody for damn sure. It may be stupid, but somebody wants it. And is willing to pay a price. Guess where you come in.'

'Where?'

He grabbed my garments. 'At the point where you tell me why somebody wants it, and who they are.'

'Golly, Kewpie,' said I, 'that sounds swell, except that I don't know what you're talking ab—'

Grunch.

His knuckles contacted the bridge of my nose. 'You tell me! You tell me what that stuff means or I'll draw it out of you in little pieces. I'm on my uppers, buddy. I got my ass kicked out of Stardust Heaven, and all my revenues cut off, and I'm in no mood to clown. You give me the dope or you've had it. And I mean now.'

He marched over, opened the case, took out a handful of papers and flung them in my lap.

My pinkies were trembling as I gathered up the sheets and gave them a quick lamp. They were typed on a typewriter with unclean keys, and I had a second or two in which to note how the sales figures were set up on the page and spaced and so forth. Then, back at the back of my somewhat terrified skull, a little plan began to wiggle into the light.

163

I handed the sheaf of stuff back to Kewpie, stood up, spread my hands in the air, failure-wise.

'Sorry, Kewpie. I'm as much up the creek as you. I don't know what it means.'

The hoodlum sighed. 'O.K., Fogel. Get to work.'

'Will I ever!' said the goon from behind, and seized my Brooks fabric.

I jerked away. 'Hold on. You didn't give me a chance to tell you the rest.' Now I was conning, conning hard and desperately. 'I've been hustling after those papers myself, Kewpie. And I mean it when I say I don't know a damn thing about what they mean. But—don't slug me, Fogel—I can send you boys to the right person, and the right place, at the right time. I can fix it up so you can collect the eighty-five grand somebody is willing to pay, don't ask me why.'

Kewpie smirked. 'You can tell me, huh? So where does that get you?'

'You'll find out. I mean to strike a bargain.'

'Balls on bargains!' Kewpie cried. 'We'll get it out of you, Havoc. Who wants the stuff? When? Where?'

'You won't get a blooming thing out of me, North, not one blooming thing, I promise! Except the tightest mouth you ever saw, if you sic your pugs on me. Because then I'll clam up. If I talk, I want something in exchange. It hurts me, Kewpie, to have to

164

give up eighty-five thousand in pure profit, but I will, provided. Provided you hold up your end.' And I handed him a marble glare which I hoped would put the convincer on it.

He studied me. Then, while Judy continued to look shaken by the whole business, Kewpie said, 'What's the deal?'

'Simple. I tell you what you want to know. Not what the stuff is. I don't know that. But who wants it. When. I give you all the dope I've got, and Judy stays here with me. Alive. Both of us alive, Kewpie, free and clear.'

Suspicion glittered in his eye, causing me to rush on.

'For God's sake, Kewpie, do you think I'd be conning you with my life at stake? I like dough, but I prefer breathing. Well? Is it a deal?'

'You and the broad alive, huh?' He scowled. My heart went hammer-hammer. 'Yeah, O.K.'

'There's a dame named Aloha Ross.'

'Hostess at The Bamboo Grove. I heard of her.'

'Well, she'll be waiting for me this afternoon at Stardust Heaven. That's right, your old place. At two o'clock this afternoon. I told her I'd be there with the case, because I figured on having it. If you turn up instead, there'll be no questions, and she'll hand over eighty-five grand in cash.'

I went over the same story several more

times without stopping, embellishing it with veiled references to Aloha's background in international intrigue, and watching Kewpie's expression change from disbelief to uncertainty to what-the-hell, he-must-be-telling-the-truth. At last, he was practically smiling as I repeated, 'Stardust Heaven. Two o'clock. Aloha Ross. She's a good-looking doll, you can't miss her.'

And maybe, I thought with ghoulish glee, she won't miss you either. Aloha had no cash to pay anybody. Kewpie would show up with the case, and let the best bunch of marksmen win once they discovered everybody was conning everybody else. Hopefully, they'd shoot it out and eliminate each other. Or at least get themselves arrested.

'Hammock,' said Kewpie, 'at last you've talked sense. I'll just take that case and—'

The front door crashed open.

Panting, Cyrus and the other thug from the porch rushed in. 'Kewpie!' Cyrus screeched. 'We're in for it! There's two or three jeep loads of sojers coming down the road. Guys with tommy guns and those green berets. I think they've got a couple of generals with them, too.'

Kewpie fanned back his sleeve. 'Oh, God. It's noon. Those God-damned war games. Okay, let's get moving.' He snapped the attaché case shut. 'We'll move out the back way. But orderly, orderly! Fogel, you and

166

Buster take care of the runt and the broad. Bring them along and make it snappy.'

'Bring us along!' I exclaimed. 'Wait a minute! You agreed—'

'Aw, come on, Hammock.' His ratfink smile widened. 'Did you really think I'd let you and the bimbo hang around here to tip the troops? I'm just gonna haul you along to Stardust Heaven, both of you. And if things work out like you promised, why, maybe I'll let you go ... after I'm on the plane out of this part of the country. But if you've told me any big fat lies, little man, you'll be personally in attendance to pay for it.'

My stars! Total failure! I had conned and lost.

I kicked my mental posterior for trusting a man of Kewpie's desperate ilk, but that did no good now. If he took us to Stardust Heaven, we would encounter Inch and Aloha fully armed, and God knew who'd get plugged.

The hoods were stirring, hustling out toward the back porch. Buster already had the arm on Judy. She looked ready to burst into tears again. Desperately I thought and thought about how to escape, or at least change the odds. Out on the dirt road, jeep engines snarled. Fogel's fingers closed on my elbow.

'Pick them up and lay them down, little man. Move!'

167

'Yes, but I've got to tie my shoelace first.'

'Make it snappy.'

I bent over, stamped on his foot, and while he let out a howl, I knocked him in the gub.

I charged past another of Kewpie's startled gunmen and frantically pried the lid of the big old leather-bound trunk lying in the corner with the rest of the junk. Small favors! There was a large strap on the inside of the lid. I hopped inside the trunk and pulled the lid down and held onto the strap for all I was worth.

Somewhere I heard Judy let out a stricken cry.

'Oh, and I thought he was so brave! Why ... why, he's just ... just a coward!'

That hurt. But no worse than Kewpie's *sotto voce* cries, of, 'For Chrissake! Get him outa there!'

The lid lurched. I coughed in the dusty confinement and held tightly to the strap. The noise of jeep motors cut out. Voices sounded outside. Heavy boots tramped. Kewpie was going, 'Oh my God, oh my God.' And then came a booming basso profundo.

'Say, there, Colonel, what the hell is all that shuffling and bumping inside this house?'

'We'll soon find out, General Offenbach,' came the reply.

Holy tomato! General D. D. (Dum-Dum) Offenbach, personal representative of the

168

Joint Chiefs, had arrived.

Soldiers outside, crooks inside, and me in the trunk. In another few seconds, I firmly expected to hear the guns going off in what looked to be a small, but fatal, war.

CHAPTER FOURTEEN

Fogel's charming voice filtered into the musty trunk.

'Gimme that heater, Rix. I'll leave them have it through the window.'

'No, no!' Kewpie hissed.

There seemed to be a great deal of grunting, knocking and whispering on the outside of my own little world of the motheaten trunk. I hung onto the lid strap with both paws, crouched uncomfortably in total black and wanting to sneeze. I couldn't hear Judy any more, but I could imagine the look of horror on her face at seeing her champion dart for cover.

Kewpie's voice came through again, strident.

'Fogel! Did you hear me? Put that rod away! We can't go around shooting U.S. government sojers! All of you stash the rods! Somebody gimme that black case. Okay, now I'm going outside and—'

A stiff knocking. 'Open up in there! Open

up! This is official military business.'

'Remember, no cannons!' Kewpie snarled. 'And get that midget out of the trunk!'

The lid gave a lurch.

A crack of light appeared around its edge.

I hung onto the strap with all my weight while Rix and Buster strained and heaved. 'The (*puff*) little (*puff*) bastid (*puff*) must (*puff*) have fixed it with (*puff*) glue. He don't look (*puff*) that strong.'

'Quiet,' said his companion, and the lid tugging stopped. 'Kewpie's goin' out.'

Blending with the tail of that sentence, came a high-pitched squeak, monosyllabic, which just might have been Judy uttering the first letter of the word help at the top of her lungs. 'Bust 'er, Fogel!' somebody hissed.

There was a grunt. A gasp. A thud.

'Beautiful, Fogel! Right on the button.'

Oh, the slimy cowards.

Fogel was puffing heavily: 'Help ... me ... carry her, you guys. We'll stash her in the trunk of the car. Get moving. Ankle it!'

Above this speech came the rattle of a bolt, the scree of a rusty screen, and a sudden increase in the babble of masculine voices outside, over which the putter of jeep engines and the crackle of a radio made a counterpoint.

'It took you long enough to open up,' said a brisk, authoritative party whose voice I recognized as that of the colonel who had

170

spoken a short while back. 'Now just what the hell are you doing on these premises mister? I'm Colonel Afferton from Fort Parnell.'

What a change in old Kewpie. He practically bubbled with fright: 'Yes, sir, your military . . . I mean your colonel-ship . . . uh, that is . . . yeah, well, I can explain.'

'And you had damn well better make it fast!' another voice put in.

'This,' said Colonel Afferton pregnantly, 'is General Offenbach.' A pause. 'From Washington.' Pause. 'The Joint Chiefs. Of Staff. Ah, a light dawns. Well, that's nice, that's very nice. It's certainly heartwarming to discover we're dealing with an intelligent civilian population.' Colonel Afferton lost his acid sense of humor. 'Mister, I don't know who you are, but you and those friends of yours I see milling around inside had better get the hell off this property. It's now almost noon. In another few minutes, these woods are going to be full of men. Shooting. Shooting live bullets. And we've requisitioned this house as an information post. For General Offenbach,' he added as a clincher.

I had gotten so interested in the conversation, I nearly forgot to hang onto the lid strap. Suddenly the lid flew up about three inches. I had a thrilling view of one of Fogel's pop eyes lamping me through the crack.

'Come out of there, you sneaky little craphead!' he hissed. 'Quick, Rix! Get your fingers under the lid!'

Rix, the good fellow, did as directed. I waited until he had a good grip on the lid, then pulled with all my might.

Rix squealed as the lid came down. Fogel shushed him apoplectically. Darkness re-fell inside the trunk. I held onto the strap, panting and sweating.

'While we're discussing it,' the Colonel was saying, 'would you mind telling us just exactly what you and your friends are doing here, mister?'

The dialogue was difficult to get complete, because Fogel & Friends were pulling, hauling and tussling with the trunk. It moved a few inches this way, a few inches that way. I heard grunts, curses, but the uglies were kept from making too much noise by the presence of the military on the porch. As I hung onto the strap for dear life, my hands began to grow numb.

Kewpie was bumbling ahead with an explanation. 'Uh, you see your military ... I mean, uh, sir, it's my cousin. My cousin owns this house.'

'What's his name?' the Colonel snapped.

'Why, uh, Brummel. We didn't know anything was coming off, officers. My cousin told me it'd be O.K. if me and my friends came out here for a little beer and poker last night. We were just gettin' ready to leave.'

'Well, hurry up!' the Colonel snapped. 'We have written authorization. Here, look at this. It says clearly that we are authorized by the owners of the property to use the entire area as an observation post during our war games.'

Rather stuffily, I thought, General Offenbach commented, 'I certainly didn't fly all the way out here to observe someone picking up poker chips and beer cans.'

'Glad to oblige, glad to oblige you fellas,' Kewpie kept burbling. 'Guess my cousin forgot to tell me about your games. We'll get going right away. Excuse me.' The screen door shut. Kewpie's voice went down low, much closer. 'For God's sakes haven't you got him out yet?'

'We tried, boss,' Fogel whined.

'O.K., then pick up the damn thing and carry it.'

Cooked!

One end of the trunk elevated. Men grunted. The sound of jeeps arriving increased. The screen door slammed.

'Just what the rinkydink hell are you people doing?' the Colonel exclaimed. 'I thought we told you to clear out.'

The trunk hit the floor. 'Uh,' said Kewpie, 'we were just moving a few odds and ends of—'

'You are not moving a damn thing, mister.'

'But ...' Kewpie said. 'Our poker chips

... our beer...'

'Leave that trunk alone and get off these premises! As you can plainly see by this watch, it is now 12:01 p.m., and as of one minute ago, this house became Army property until the conclusion of the games. Now if you clowns don't hustle, I'll call my MPs and have you all arrested by the civil cops. Believe me, this whole set-up is mighty suspicious anyway. A bunch of grown men sitting around in the woods like the three bears. It stinks. I just don't have time to worry about it, or I would. Now are you going or do I whistle for the MPs?'

That did it. 'We're going, we're going, your officer ... I mean, we're going,' Kewpie cried.

And there I was, alone in my little gray trunk in the west, trying to keep from sneezing and weeping with remorse at the same time.

I heard a door slam. A few seconds later, a motor turned over. Gunned. Receded, out behind the house.

Heavy boots thudded. Soldiers started jawing and making a lot of clatter. A shot rang out, far away, another. The Colonel said, 'Hurry up with that radio equipment! We're behind schedule.'

They weren't the only ones.

My schedule called for trying to pull Judy Swanson from the clutches of the Kewpie

174

Mob. I was free, in a loose manner of speaking, but probably miles from Judy already. I had a whole damn maneuvering army blocking my way. I didn't even know for sure whether Kewpie would head for Stardust Heaven at two, in just a little under two hours. But if he did, and if he dragged Judy, that was real trouble.

I had to get out of the trunk.

But I didn't quite have enough nerve yet. I tried to work up some.

The racket continued outside in the parlor. Metallic clankings. Whistlings and whee-wheeings, as though radio bands were being tuned in. Then a voice crackled:

'This is Swiss Cheese! This is Swiss Cheese! Hello Swiss Cheese Hole Forty-Three, how do you read me?' Abruptly someone switched down the gain. Another voice came through a speaker, sounding frantic.

'Distributor Cap to all sparkplugs, Distributor Cap to all sparkplugs!'

The Colonel's voice intervened. 'Distributor Cap is the Blue army, General.'

'Um, garrum, yes,' said Dum-Dum sagely. 'And Swiss Cheese the Red?'

'Correct. Each of the two armies in the game, the Red and the Blue has its own channel code signal. But with this equipment, we can listen in and monitor both of them. When we get some heavy action, you can tell what's happening, and we'll drive you to forward observation.'

Swiss Cheese for the Red army, Distributor Cap for the Blue. All very interesting, but not helping me a damn bit.

Except for the roar of an approaching jeep, it was momentarily quiet outside. Shots rang again, and then became distressingly frequent. I had to make a move.

I did, by raising the lid.

I got a peep at them before they saw me—half a dozen noncoms at a hastily-rigged radio panel along one wall. And the Colonel, and General Offenbach himself, the latter with plum-colored jowls, silvery hair and spotless uniform. He was the first to see me, turning a boiled eye toward the front door and by chance spotting my rising from the interior of the trunk.

'My God, Colonel! Look!'

'Say,' I said as I stepped out, 'I must have slept through the poker game.' I started ankling toward the hall which led to the back door. 'Sorry about that fellas, but I was carrying quite a load last night. I'll get out of your hair right away.'

The noncoms manning the radio equipment had their heads screwed around in surprise, and for a moment more the advantage was mine, but only for a moment. That blamed jeep I'd heard approaching stopped out in front. Feet clattered. The door opened. I goggled in acute horror.

'Sorry I'm late, General. We ran into ... you! Y—y—you! Arrest him hold him, grab him!'

And there was mighty wrath, and big trouble for me, in the outstretched, shaking finger of that fearless military leader, Major General Morris Bark.

CHAPTER FIFTEEN

General Dum-Dum Offenbach turned assorted shades of maroon. 'Bark, what in the ringding-dong, red-tailed, fire-eating hell is going on in these damn maneuvers of yours? Civilians, civilians everywhere! Playing poker in the command post! Popping out of trunks! Who is this man?'

'An escaped criminal,' Bark panted, lunging.

I lunged the other way. General Offenbach executed a mastodon-like step which placed him in the doorway leading to the rear exit.

'Watch it, butterball!' cried I. 'You're blocking the egress!' I lowered my head and gave him a butt in the corporation.

He tumbled pratt over epaulets. Bark screamed, 'Oh my God, the little bastard assaulted Joint Chiefs!'

'Leggo my ankle, fatty!' I was exclaiming,

177

as Offenbach seized hold. I gave my leg a wrench. Dum-Dum's hand flew loose and the knuckles smacked painfully against the wall.

'You'll ... hear about this ... Bark,' he was burbling. 'From ... Washington ... I promise...'

I scuttled back through the kitchen. Poor General Bark did not know whether to pursue me or assist Dum-Dum in regaining his feet. He chose the latter. His noncoms were trying to do eighteen jobs at once—monitor radio traffic, respond to his cries to help Dum-Dum, and catch me, among others. Offenbach was still blocking the doorway, however. I zipped out the back door of the house, across the dirt driveway and into the trees.

I ran for about five minutes, then stopped, panting.

Off to the left I heard vague clankings and clatterings. I didn't want to contemplate what had happened back at the Brummel Place because, in all my numerous assaults upon the law, I had never pulled off anything to match a physical attack upon the person of a representative of the Joint Chiefs. I felt a little like I had taken a piece of chalk and scrawled 'Martha was a fink' on the base of the Washington Monument.

I rested against a tree. A peculiar whistling noise arose in the forest to the left. Curious, I looked that way, mumbling, 'That's the funniest darn whistling sound I ever—'

The tree trunk directly above my head exploded in a cloud of white smoke. There was a big blam.

I threw myself forward on the turf as branches rained down. The war games had begun in earnest.

Another shell came in. Another tree disappeared. Zip, zow, zam. Three more trees were disposed of while I lay like a jelly on the ground and watched the approach of the vehicle which was firing the shells to clear a hasty path through the woods.

It was a large, open weapons-carrier, with a snip of red cloth tied around its radio mast to identify it as part of the Red army. Several tough apples in field clothes and green berets crouched inside while the commander of the vehicle stood up in front shouting:

'Now that one, Rappaport! Blast it! We'll encircle the enemy yet.'

I tried to think of something to use for a white flag. No time to take off my shirt. So I hopped up and just waved my arms. The weapons carrier veered. The large, long-muzzled piece of artillery in the front rotated. I realized with dismay that the next tree which they wished to remove was directly behind me.

'Stop, stop! I surrender!'

The infernal machine clanked on. The gunner was calling range and elevation.

'Wait, wait, I'm a civilian!'

'Look!' a soldier shouted. 'There's a guy out there.'

'My car broke down!' I shouted. 'I lost my road map. Point that thing somewhere else.'

'Hold your fire!' cried the vehicle's commander, a lieutenant. He peered ahead. Then he straightened up. 'It's a trick, men. The Blues are sending out guerillas in mufti. Take that man prisoner!'

Out of the carrier piled three of the toughies. They advanced, weapons ready. 'You're caught,' one said.

'I'm just looking for the superhighway,' I exclaimed, moving fast. I dodged around the trio, jumped high, caught the barrel of the cannon extending over the front of the vehicle, vaulted up and over and landed inside, smack against the lieutenant. While he cursed, I stepped on his combat ribbons and jumped off the other side of the vehicle before anybody could grab me.

I cut to the right through the trees. I ran for about ten minutes, then stopped to rest again. There seemed to be no pursuit. But how much longer could I dodge around in this woodsy setting without getting blasted, arrested, incarcerated or otherwise damaged?

Three smoke bombs lobbed in from overhead, whistling down and smashing within six yards of me. One was red, the second blue, the third white. By the time I

180

got out of there, my lungs were full of patriotic fumes and I was coughing like crazy.

After I reeled out of the smoke, I noticed that the woods seemed to thin out a bit ahead. I had a fleeting vista of a sloping meadow, blue sky peppered with the white puffs of exploding shells. Men ran every which way. A tank rumbled against the skyline.

At least in the open I would be able to see what was coming at me. I stumbled along, left the trees behind, and had gone maybe a hundred yards when a cry rang out from the tall weeds:

'Infiltrators ready! Charge!'

Up out of the shrubbery sprang a dozen, two dozen ... three dozen! They were in combat gear, with pieces of blue ribbon pinned to the berets. Each one had a rifle with a shiny bayonet on the end. They charged toward the woods with all sorts of wild cries, yells and oaths ringing out.

Their commander, a tiger in a lacquered helmet, followed them on the run, shouting, 'That's it, that's it. And if you see any Reds, men ... rip their guts out!'

Of course in war games, nobody would seriously think of ripping anybody else's guts out.

Would they?

They swept toward me. I turned around.

That was when I saw the eight tanks coming up, tracks spinning in the loamy soil.

Little red pennons fluttered from the radio masts.

'I see a Red skirmisher!' shouted one of the lads rushing toward me.

'Where?' I said. Then I realized he meant me. 'Hey! Hey, you guys. Hold it a second! I'm lost. I'm not—'

'There's one!' the lacquer-headed commander bawled. 'Get him!'

Before I could think of what to do, a smoke shell lobbed by the tank exploded on my left. Another burst on the right. The Blue troops began to curse, suddenly hidden by the reeking white stuff drifting all around. It was the tanks or the troops. I picked the troops. I would try to get through the steadily advancing line.

'Ow, damn it!' somebody yelled as I crashed against him. I felt cold steel shave past my left cheek. The Blue into whom I had blundered began to flail at me.

'Retreat, retreat!' I shouted. 'We're totally surrounded?'

'Who is it, who is it?' somebody yelled through the murk. 'Is that you, Flattley?'

'Yeah, it's me, Flattley. And watch that bayonet. It's—oh boy!'

He accidentally pronged me in the behind with the instrument. I must have leaped a foot. From sheer defensive reaction, I took a swing at him. Missed. The momentum carried me on around. In the smoke, my

182

knuckles struck something hard.

There was an outraged cry. When I looked again, the lacquered-helmeted leader was stretched out cold.

Men continued to run around frantically. Bayonets flashed too close for comfort. On impulse, I peeled off my Brooks jacket, peeled off the leader's battle jacket, and though it was four sizes too large, managed to get it buttoned and the sleeves rolled up as I charged ahead. In a moment I had the helmet on too. From the waist up, I had a vague resemblance to a soldier.

Behind, in the trees, the Blues and Reds had joined the battle, amidst a symphony of oaths, intermixed with the whine of smoke shells, the clank of tanks treads and other sounds of martial merriment. The meadow, by contrast, seemed temporarily deserted. I got out of the smoke, glanced around, saw a company of troops half a mile off, and that was all.

The troops were working their way over the crest of a hill, approaching me. Just ahead was another low hill. I huddled in the weeds, ran up to the crest of the hill and flopped on my belly.

The sun was broiling. Insects buzzed all around in the weeds. I heard a faint mutter of voices. I wiped my dripping forehead, parted the weeds and examined the scene below.

The only military types in evidence were

the members of that company catfooting through the shrubbery on the left. They seemed to be coming toward this hill, though at a slow pace. I still heard voices. From where, I was hard put to tell.

About a mile past the field, sunlight burned and glinted off the roofs of several hundred parked autos. Beyond that, a patchwork of towers and roller coaster skeletons against the blue afternoon sky.

Funnyland. Then I had worked my way to the fringe of the battle area after all.

I examined my watch. The hands said nineteen minutes before two.

And I remembered all too well what would happen at two sharp, when the opposing parties in the mad game of espionage surprised each other at Stardust Heaven, with poor Judy right in the middle.

I had to do something.

The question was, what?

The voices came again.

'Distributor Cap Six awaiting orders, over.' That voice had a faint echo.

'This is Distributor Cap Command Post V for Valve. Hold your position and await further orders.'

That voice sounded quite close. I began to shinny forward on hands and knees. The company of troops on the left had vanished. They couldn't have marched out of sight, so they were therefore hunkered down somewhere in the weeds. Had they been the gents to which the eerie voice had been talking? Possibly.

Suddenly there was another crackling. 'Distributor Cap Two to Distributor Cap Command Post V for Valve! Captain Scroggs! They're moving in.'

'Hang on!' cried a voice, just below me, I realized. 'Where are you?'

'About three quarters of a mile on your left, over by the telephone poles.'

'What's wrong?'

'We're trying to escape with the plan maps. But we've only got three men not captured.'

'We'll be there. Corporal, you hold on here. We'll try to cut those men loose.'

And, before I could say Remember the Maine, three battle-clad shapes popped up out of the weeds down at the bottom of the hill.

Clutching their berets, they went pelting off through the foliage. I goggled. A crackling voice on the radio issued another frantic call for Captain Scroggs, to which a pip-squeak reply cheeped out of the little burrow into which they had been dug at the bottom of this very hill.

'This is Corporal Buttolph speaking, Captain Scroggs is not here, over.'

'Well, Goddam it, where is he? This is Distributor Cap Six awaiting orders.'

'Corporal Buttolph here. You'll just have to

stay dug in until—'

'Unprintable that, Corporal,' replied the voice on the radio. 'There are some kids down in the unprintable parking lot right behind us, and they're throwing rocks. One of the little unprintables has a pea-shooter. You ought to be here to feel what the little unprintable thing can do. The range is impossible, but—ow! Get out of here, you little unprintables, this is government property!'

Right then, laid out on the top of the weed-covered hill and fairly certain by now that Distributor Cap Six was the group entrenched over on the left, I got a loony, last-chance idea.

It was a crazy and desperate way to try and pull the chestnuts out of the fire, but I was both desperate and slightly crazy by this time. I stood up.

I glanced both ways. The meadow seemed deserted still. All sorts of guns were going off back in the woods, though, and smoke was billowing there. I might make it if they kept busy.

Emiting what I thought was a war-crazed yell, I went tearing down the slope.

'Hands up, surrender, you're surrounded!' I hollered, able by now to see the lone corporal squatted in the burrow they'd trenched. He owled me with thick glasses and started to exclaim, just as I launched myself

186

through space.

I landed on top of Corporal Buttolph, who tried to paste me with his walkie-talkie. I struck first. Right on the jaw.

He tumbled in a heap.

'Get up,' I said.

He did, glasses hanging by one earpiece. 'That ... that's no way to take a prisoner! You're only supposed to give a light tap on—hey! Who are you? Where'd you get that white shirt? Those slacks?'

'They couldn't find anything else my size.' I snatched up his rifle and pointed it at him. 'Start marching. I'm going to capture you.'

'I'll be court martialed for losing the command post!' he wailed.

'I'm sorry, buddy, but worse things will happen to somebody else unless I can—never mind! Start marching. Double time. Hup, two, three, four!'

Though Corporal Buttolph's heart wasn't in it, he trudged off, hands above his head.

When I was sure that he didn't intend to double back, I threw down the rifle and grabbed the walkie-talkie.

'Distributor Cap Command Post V for Valve, calling Distributor Cap Six,' I said with one hand over my mouth. I repeated the message.

'We're here, we're here,' said a voice. 'Goddam that kid with that pea-shooter. Keep down, you guys. No, you can't shoot

187

them. Is that you Captain Scroggs?'

'Right.'

'When the hell are we going to get out of here?'

'Immediately. Listen carefully. We're going to try a new plan. We're practically surrounded, so we're going to break out. Proceed to Funnyland Park immediately, and rendezvous at Stardust Heaven.'

There were garbled outcries from the other end.

'Who's doing the commanding here?' I shouted. 'You heard me! I'm going to win, and I don't give a dang how we do it! To repeat that order, proceed directly to Funnyland Park and rendezvous at Stardust Heaven. That is a direct order, and you'll carry it out on the double.'

The voice on the other end of the radio said, muffled, 'I think Captain Scroggs has flipped.'

'I heard that!' I cried. 'You'll carry out the orders at once.'

'Uh, wilco, Captain. Stardust Heaven, on the double. Chee-zuz! I mean over and out.'

I dropped the radio. Off went the helmet, the jacket, and I charged away across the meadow. Over my shoulder, I saw the troops standing up, starting to move.

I reached the parking lot and dodged between cars, running like I'd never run in my life.

I hoped to heaven the troops would move into the position given them, but I had no way of knowing. I had to go on ahead, and forestall the bloodshed, troops or not. I bounced off this car, that one. I reached the Park's main entrance. I leaped the turnstile.

'Hey, you, stop!' the guard screeched.

I kept going. The hands on my watch pointed to one minute before two o'clock.

CHAPTER SIXTEEN

A Saturday always brings out the marks. This Saturday was no exception. Crowds hustled and bustled on the streets of Funnyland, the roller coasters rattled, the shooting galleries clanged, and my loafers picked up the customary quota of old gum and popcorn hulls as I ankled along at a rapid clip. I hoped the lads of Distributor Cap Six would at least stumble far enough into the Park to create a diversion, but there was no guarantee, and I didn't waste time looking back.

By the time the cupolas and gingerbread of Stardust Heaven loomed ahead, it was five past two.

The boards nailed between the pillars and posts of the dance pavilion presented a solid, unbreachable wall. Were the menaces inside? No way to tell. I saw nobody suspicious

189

outside.

I started going from door to door, trying to look as authoritative as possible in my dirty old white shirt and beat-up Brooks pants. The door to the cocktail bar was locked tight. But the door to the short order section appeared slightly ajar.

I gave the handle a twist. The knob fell off. Feeling redder than red, I slipped the chrome object in my pocket, hoped nobody was watching too closely, and pried the door open.

I darted inside, blinking in the gloom. No sap descended to abuse my skull as I stood a second there in the dimness. Voices murmured far off to the left. It suddenly occurred to me that they probably had not bothered about lookouts because Kewpie North had every right to assume yours truly was in the hands of the military cops.

I stole along cautiously and flattened against a wall leading to a door which opened onto the boarded-up dance floor. The door was the swinging type. I squatted down and started pushing carefully with an index finger.

When the door was open about an inch, I took the knob out of my pocket and wedged it into the crack. The hall was pitch dark, but a little light filtered onto the dance floor out there through cracks in the boards. What I saw made me bite my mental nails with frantic abandon.

The lethal confrontation had already begun.

In this corner—to the left of my vantage point—Miss Aloha Ross, chicly dressed in a lightweight suit of summer linen. A scarf was tied around her dark hair. She wore white pumps, and looked like she had just stepped out of a fashion ad, except that fashion models never look as though they wanted to murder someone. Backing her up was Inch, with a cannon in his mitt.

In the other corner, on my right, Mr. Kewpie North, his pudgy hand wrapped around the handle of the silver-stamped attaché case. Backing him up, Fogel with his green suit and enlarged optics, and Lou Cyrus. Both had guns aimed at Aloha and Inch. Cyrus also had one hand on poor Judy Swanson, who looked exhausted and absolutely terrified.

'Come, come, Mr. North,' Aloha was saying in that sexy voice. She showed a lot of teeth but the smile was totally phony. She ran one hand suggestively down her hip to smooth her skirt. 'There's no reason why we should quarrel over this, even though our meeting did come as something of a surprise to me. I'd expected that little fool John Havoc to be here. Obviously he didn't think I meant it when I threatened to track him down if he failed to show up with that case.'

'I tol' you,' Kewpie said, 'Havoc is the one

who flimflammed me into coming here, lady. Now I want the dough.'

'And I,' said Aloha, just a shade nervously, 'want that attaché case.'

'Maybe I won't pass it over until I see the color of your bills,' said Kewpie.

Aloha bit her lip. Did Kewpie know that Aloha was not the party carrying the bundle? From the pause, her hesitation, I figured that he did not. And she was doubtless not about to tell him.

Instead, she gave him a lush, smoldering look. 'Can't we ... discuss this in more comfortable surroundings, Mr. North?'

'Like where?'

'Oh, I don't know. Someplace that would be a little more, shall we say, intimate?'

'I ain't got time for intimate,' Kewpie returned. 'I'm busted and I need lettuce.'

'Dear Mr. North! I could be very nice to you, if only you would—'

'Quit the goo-goo eyes routine, dolly,' Kewpie broke in. 'In my financial condition, I can't afford it.'

I was sweating plenty, wondering who would blast whom first.

Aloha tried a casual gesture. She was too tense for it. 'Mr. North, I repeat—the contents of that case will be absolutely useless to you without certain information which I alone possess.' She was doing the flimflamming now.

'Listen, babe!' Kewpie said heatedly. 'I'm tired of this stalling. That little punk Havoc said you'd pay eighty-five thousand smackers for what's in here.'

Aloha laughed even more brightly. 'Havoc said that? Little Mr. Havoc? Why, we both know Mr. Havoc can't be trusted. He's a wretched, double-crossing little swindler. Let me be perfectly honest with you. I do not have any eighty-five thousand dollars.'

Kewpie digested this. 'Then, dolly, you gonna wish you did, all the way to the funeral home. Fogel!'

'Wait!' Aloha took a step toward him.

'For what?'

She undulated her ample behind in a manner that made Kewpie's eyes light up despite his best intentions. Fogel's practically stood out on stalks. Judy looked paler than ever. Just as she looked like she might faint, Cyrus stepped on her toe and jarred her awake.

'If we quarrel, Mr. North,' Aloha purred seductively, 'there will be nothing but a lot of unpleasantness all around. Guns going off, possibly several people getting hurt ... and neither of us will profit. Believe me, I do know who wants that attaché case, and is willing to pay eighty-five thousand dollars for it. In fact, I think I could even raise the price on the spot. Demand, say one hundred thousand dollars. And get it. That would give each of us fifty thousand dollars. Remember, unless you trust me, we're both out of luck.'

A long, tense moment followed.

Kewpie whispered something to egg-eyes Fogel. Fogel gave a nod. Kewpie munched his panatella. Finally he shrugged. There was grudging admiration in his eyes as he said, 'O.K., babe. You're a first class poker player, whoever you are. Fifty-fifty it is. I know when I'm outclassed. Let's go get the kale.'

Aloha shook her head. 'We must wait until six this evening. Don't worry, neither one of us will let the other out of sight, eh? I promise everything will work.'

'Who's going to hand over the green?' Kewpie wanted to know.

'A gentleman named—'

Aloha stopped. Her gaze slid past his shoulder. And for all her slick looks, the moment her eyes lit on poor, tottering, exhausted Judy, Miss Ross looked like a witch out of a children's book.

'I won't say any more, Mr. North. Not until we dispose of possible witnesses.'

Blinking owlishly, Kewpie turned to stare at Judy. Cyrus said, 'It's okay by me, boss. I've had enough of this cheating little broad.'

'Well, it isn't okay by me,' Kewpie snapped. And for the first time, it became evident who played in the major leagues, and who in the minors. Mr. Kewpie was strictly second string when it came to homicide.

'Listen, babe, I don't pull off a chill on no female's say-so. In fact, I don't like to pull off a chill, period. I don't mind busting a few bones, or snapping off some guy's fingers or giving him a fracture in the head with a sap. That's all part of the business. But murder? Lady, murder gets you fried.'

'You've made up your mind about that, have you?' Aloha purred.

'Yeah,' Kewpie said.

I breathed easier.

'I think so,' Kewpie said.

I stopped breathing.

'You'll have to do more than think so,' Aloha said. 'Because I refuse to play at all while we have a witness left alive. Your men are one thing. But that girl . . .' Like someone swatting a fly, casually, Aloha shook her head. 'She has to go.'

Kewpie hefted the attaché case. 'I dunno. It's pretty far out.'

'Unless you do it,' Aloha said, 'the fifty thousand dollars will never be yours.'

Poor Kewpie looked miserable, and damn his penny-ante soul, less certain as he said, 'Look, are you sure there ain't any other way?'

'Let me explain exactly why I'm positive,' Aloha said in a friendly, persuasive voice. And she began to give him a long rigmarole, most of which I failed to hear because I was in a total state of panic.

195

Where the devil was the commotion those soldiers from Fort Percy Parnell were supposed to cause by their arrival, thereby giving me a chance to dart in and take a hand? All I could hear was the regular racket of the Park. Aloha's voice purred on and on, persuading, persuading, and now Lou Cyrus chimed in with a nod, and agreement, and Kewpie, weakening, said, 'Yeah, I see that point. But I'm still not sure...'

Aloha was practically on top of him, smiling and bumping her hip against him and even giving him a little tweak on the ear. If only the damn soldiers would arrive!

When they did, there'd be enough distraction for me to take a chance on reaching Judy. From where I was crouched in the hallway, it was a long, long way out to the center of the dance floor where the confab was taking place. Not being armed with a cannon, I would be plugged before I got half way out there. The next thing somebody would do after they shot me was to figure the game was really up, and blast Judy fast.

'Nah,' Kewpie said, 'I still don't like it.'

'You imbec—' Aloha began, then forced it back and smiled. 'North, be reasonable! We both stand to benefit.'

'But I stand to get the hoosegow for life if we remove the doll and we're caught.'

'I'll have my man Inch do it, for heaven's sake!'

196

'Same difference,' said Kewpie.

Aloha wouldn't give up. She started persuading again, this time applying more portions of her anatomy to Kewpie's, going bump, bump, and bang and tickle and pinch. Kewpie had lost the earlier round and he was sure to lose this one, because she was a murder machine and he was just a poor, dumb hoodlum.

Should I run out there and attack them?

No, that would finish Judy for sure. I had to see what had happened to those damn troops.

Finally I faced up to the choice. Try to charge them like the one-man cavalry, which was a stupid and a losing gambit. Or leave Stardust Heaven for a few minutes, and take the chance Aloha wouldn't win Kewpie North over too fast, and get Judy plugged before I returned.

'Stay alive, sweetie,' I whispered fervently to the dark air of the hall. I took a last look at her, removed the doorknob from the crack, crawled away and ran like crazy for the outside.

CHAPTER SEVENTEEN

Outside Stardust Heaven, crowds jammed the Park streets. Spectacles of carefree merriment and weekend abandon greeted the eye on every hand, and all I could think about was Judy, Judy, poor Judy, under the gun back inside the dance hall. I looked every which way, straining for a sign of those troops of the Blue army I thought I had misdirected into the Park.

Not a soldier in sight anywh—

I was wrong!

Down one of the streets fanning out from the wide asphalt area in front of Stardust Heaven, I glimpsed a glimmer of green beret above the passing crowd.

A woman and man came huffing along. The broad was complaining. 'Well, Chesley, all I can say is, the juvenile delinquent problem has certainly gotten out of hand when they have to call in soldiers to handle it!'

The troops were about half a block off. They seemed to be milling around. I heard a few colorful curses during a lull in crowd noise. A rifle glinted. I rushed in that direction.

Right in the middle of the thoroughfare, the soldiers were standing around and staring blankly at one another while the lieutenant obviously in charge consulted a military map. One corporal reached down to scratch the top of his paratrooper's boot, said, 'Say, Loot, what the hell's coming off here anyway?'

'I wish I knew,' replied the miserable

officer. 'The orders were, surround Stardust Heaven. That's that place up ahead. i think Captain Scroggs must have gone round the bend. There's nothing around here but civilians.'

I, meantime, was skulking behind a wheeled stand whose proprietor vended caramel-coated candy apples.

'I think we better pull a strategic retreat,' said the lieutenant. A hand seized my shoulder.

I found myself gazing into the mustachioed face of the apple-stand owner.

'You wanna buy somepin, sonny, or you no wanna buy?'

'Actually, I was just looking—' I began. Then came the flash.

The lieutenant, conferring with a couple of his noncoms, was pointedly ignoring some hoots and jeers cast by a couple of teenagers on the far side of the crowd. Abruptly the lieutenant pointed back in the direction of Fort Percy Parnell.

'We'll go that way. Fall in, fall in, you men! Let's make this orderly!'

The troops began to assemble themselves. I had to get those boys moving, and quick. But in the right direction. And to help to do it, I had just remembered a casual remark passed off by major General Morris Bark, concerning what riled his men the most.

'How much for some of these apples,

mister?' I said.

'Ten cents apiece, kid. Whatsamatter, you no can read the sign?'

Rapidly I counted the apples in two cardboard trays. 'I'll take two trays. Let's see, that's two dollars. Here.'

Thrusting practically my last two bills into his hand, I darted off with the trays. In the middle of the street, I set the trays on top of a drinking fountain temporarily deserted by moppets and picked up two of the apples.

The caramel coatings sort of stuck, but I managed to lob them both pretty well. As they sailed through the air, I began hollering:

'Yoo hoo, oh yoo hoo!'

'Forward, march!' the lieutenant shouted, just as he got a candy apple in the puss.

Dripping caramel, he let out a yell. The second missile struck him just behind the ear. I hollered louder.

'Yoo hoo, sojers! Oh you big crazy sojers, yoo hoo!'

One of the ferocious-looking boys in the rear rank swung around, saw me, glared. 'A civilian wiseguy. You watch your mouth, sonny!'

'Where'd you get those pretty green hats?' I piped.

The soldier's face reddened. 'You be careful, you lousy little—'

'Tell me, tell me, where'd you get those darling green hats, girls?'

'Bastaaaaaard!' shouted the red-faced soldier, and broke ranks on the run.

'At ease!' shouted the confused lieutenant. 'Steady! Hold your fire! As you were!' I let him have another candy apple in the chops. Then I began pelting them in amongst the regulars, blop, blop, blop, and hurling more insults along with them: 'Who's your milliner, sweetheart? Yoo hoo!'

'Get him, get him!' the tough types started crying. Civilians began to yell. A riot was brewing.

'Gotta catch me first!' I yelled, and ran.

The soldiers all broke formation despite the lieutenant's caterwauling. I zipped in and out of the crowd as the disorganized troop rushed in pursuit. I cut this way, that way, leaped a pram crying, 'Yoo hoo, yoo hoo!' for all I was worth.

Crash! I smacked against the door of Stardust Heaven, ripped inside, hid under a table in the short order restaurant.

Troops piled inside.

'Get him!'

'Where'd he go?'

'Let's catch the creep and teach him a lesson!'

The lieutenant stuck his head in. 'Outside, outside, you men! The civilians are attacking!'

From my vantage point, I could see it was true. Several of the running soldiers must have bumped pedestrians and fists had started swinging. I saw a man in a sport shirt go flying by the open door, six feet above the ground. There were assorted crunching and pulping sounds, and then the milling men in the doorway hid everything.

Suddenly, down the corridor from the boarded-up dance floor, a massive shape came lumbering.

Inch, with cannon in hand.

'What is goin' on out here anyway?' He gaped. Then, over his shoulder: 'Run for it, Miss Ross! There's some kind of riot!'

That's when I came bouncing up from beneath the table, snagged the sugar bowl and let him have it.

The chinaware contacted his nose. He stumbled against the wall. 'There he goes!' a soldier shouted as I leapfrogged Inch's floundering carcass, pelted down the hall and skidded out on the waxed boards of the dance floor, yelling, 'It's a riot, a riot!'

The scene froze, an assortment of faces registering various degrees of distress. All I was concerned about was one—Judy's. She was peering at me with consternation, still beautifully alive.

'It's a Goddam sellout!' Kewpie North exclaimed, pulling his cannon from the waistband of his pants. Inch was up, stumbling down the hall after me, and just a few steps ahead of the troops.

'Inch!' Aloha shrieked. 'Take care of them! We've been double-crossed!'

'Down, Judy!' I bawled, diving. I hit her in the lower calf region as Inch's first shot went off.

It racketed like thunder in the closed, stuffy pavilion. Lou Cyrus let out a yell, clutched his middle, flipped over. I heard Inch chuckle loudly. Fogel had his own heater out, was spinning around. Inch fired again.

Fogel's eyes stuck out further than ever. He looked like a hideous Christmas decoration with that red patch of gore blooming on the breast pocket of his green suit. Down he tumbled.

'The little one! Kill him, Inch!'

That was Aloha. The rage and dismay in her voice were raw, brutal. I was floundering on top of Judy, trying to get up. Troops poured onto the dance floor, but the situation was still too confused for them to be of much help in the next few seconds. I saw Fogel's heater lying about two feet away, went crawling toward it.

I got my hands around the butt as Aloha kept screaming. I twisted onto my back. Judy woke up, added her shrieks to the din, just as Inch came charging toward me, face working, cannon muzzle pointed at my belly.

Desperately I hefted Fogel's gun, triggered it.

203

Inch's hand worked even after the slug hit him in the chest. As he fell, his gun went off. A bullet plowed a channel in the wood half an inch from me.

Behind, I heard a terrific banging and hammering. I staggered up, spun. Mr. Kewpie North was attempting to beat his way out of the pavilion by smashing the black attaché case against the boards nailed to the outside of the pillars. He already had two of the planks dislodged. Sunlight poured in.

I dove for him, hit him around the legs and brought him down. I dodged the hand with which he tried to brain me with the cannon. I stamped on his wrist, jumped up and down on his midriff, tore the attaché case out of his hands and panted for breath.

I turned around again. And went cold.

Aloha Ross had produced a small nickeled revolver from somewhere. Trapped, with soldiers milling behind her, she was glaring at me. A mad, mad glare of fury. But she was aiming the pistol at Judy, still sprawled in a daze.

Aloha's dark eyes said the last thing she would do to me—and because of me—would be to kill Judy.

It was a choice between the cannon or the case. Because I thought somebody might want her alive, I chose the case. I drew back, sailed it through the air.

Aloha cursed, a dirty, dirty curse. She

pulled the trigger just as the case hit her shoulder. She spun around, the gun barked, the bullet plowed into the wall and Judy screamed again.

When they pulled me off, I was attempting to clobber Aloha with a most ungentlemanly punch.

'Take everything into custody! All the guns, that case, everything!' the lieutenant was bawling as he pushed through into the confusion. A soldier helped himself to Aloha's revolver lying on the floor. Another glommed onto the attaché case. Out of breath, all I could do was gargle helplessly.

Judy tottered up. She rushed to my side. I found enough strength to put my arm around her. Several of the troops had Kewpie under control. Others collected Aloha and kept her quiet.

'Everybody,' said the lieutenant, 'but everybody, is under military arrest.'

'You don't understand,' I began.

'Oh, don't I?' returned the loot, fingering candy apple caramel stuck in his eyebrows. I had a vast stinking feeling in my middle as I watched the fingers of one of the burly-boys curl tighter around the handle of the black attaché case. Goodbye, eighty-five thousand clams. All that work, sweat and blood for nothing.

The lieutenant was ordering one of his noncoms to find a phone on the double.

'Lieutenant,' I said, 'they were going to kill this poor girl here. They're spies and crooks and ... I had to get you guys here with the candy apple routine, or they'd have—'

'Shut up!' he said loudly.

Shuddering, Judy hugged me. 'Johnny ... Johnny, I thought I was done for a minute ago.'

'Nearly, hon.' I watched the attaché case disappear out the door. Oh, woe!

'Let's get moving, you people,' said the noncom who prodded me.

'Wait, wait!' I exclaimed. 'I tell you that woman they're taking out is a spy who—'

'Sure, pal,' he said patronizingly. 'Sure, and I'm Orphan Annie. Haul it!'

Is that any way for a patriot to be treated?

But I got treated that way all the same.

CHAPTER EIGHTEEN

'But I tell you guys for the ninety-ninth time,' I said. 'I am innocent.'

'Stop,' said Detective First Grade FitzHugh Goodpasture. 'Stop before I double over with mirth.'

'Innocent!' Major General Morris Bark sounded like a leaky steam valve as he sputtered. 'My God! The gall! Innocent! Damaging government property!

Demoralizing federal troops! Inciting a riot! Posing as an officer! Giving my boys a bad press as the result of the fracas with the civilians at Funnyland!' Bark quivered in front of me. 'Have you seen the photo plastered all over the front page of the evening paper, you little ... saboteur?'

'No,' I said meekly.

'It shows Lieutenant Beemis, one of my best men, with a candy apple stuck to his beret, Goddammit! Great for morale! Just great!'

The scene of this miscarriage of justice was a small office in the county sheriff's sub-station not far from Funnyland. Goodpasture, rushing out from the city, had commandeered the quarters, and proceeded to wring me out. Through the window, twilight was deepening. The sunset sparkled on the waters off the South Shore. Inside the office, I reposed in a wooden chair which hurt my sacroiliac.

'For the last time, Havoc!' Goodpasture howled. 'Confess!'

I sighed. 'But I have been over it and over it, Fitz. I have told you why everything I did was absolutely necessary not only for national security but to save Miss Swanson's life. When the story hits the paper, public opinion will vindicate me.' I didn't believe it for a second. This time, I was really fried.

Wearing combat clothes, General Bark

perched on the corner of a desk, glowered. 'Well, that is one place where you are wrong, Havoc. Washington has taken a hand.'

'Washington?'

'Affirmative. Although the facts about that ... that massacre at Stardust Heaven will be in the papers, the significance of the events will be hushed up. So don't go looking for any sob-sisters to start calling you another Nathan Hale.'

'Nathan Hale was hung,' I said.

'Yes.' Bark smiled. 'Isn't that the truth?'

FitzHugh began to wave his moist cigar. 'Of course you caught a dangerous foreign agent in the person of that Miss Ross. But look what you did in the process!' He ticked off on his fingers. 'Mayhem, assault, corpses, public property damage. Why, Havoc, you're a worse menace to the American way than fifty enemy agents!'

Bark coughed. 'All right, Goodpasture, all right. Oratory is one thing. But let's be practical. Precisely what charges are you going to bring against Havoc here?'

FitzHugh glowered. 'Enough to put him away almost for life, don't you worry. I phoned the D.A.'s office on the way out here. He had half his staff combing the penal code. Believe me, Havoc, sometimes the law works in devious ways its services to perform, but we intend to nail you on every dusty, musty rap we can dig up. It's time we removed a

208

menace like you from circulation. I promise, before we're through, we'll...'

On and on he droned, cataloguing my dismal future. I can't say I blamed him, but the picture he painted was still pretty depressing.

'FitzHugh?' I said. 'Is it all right if I light a cigarette?'

'No, it is not! You sit there and listen to—'

The door crashed open.

'Everybody's been giving me the damned runaround,' a voice boomed, 'and I'm sick of it! Now where is that little ... oh, there you are!'

'General Offenbach!' I cried. 'Oh, cripes.'

Looking like someone had snipped his hot line behind his back, General Dum-Dum Offenbach stalked in. His face was like a sky full of thunderclouds. Bark appeared to grow faint. Goodpasture practically snapped to attention. Here it comes, I thought. The Joint Chiefs will probably hang me for butting Dum-Dum in his paunch, which right now seemed to be quaking as a visible sign of his annoyance.

After scowling ferociously for the better part of thirty seconds, Dum-Dum swung toward me.

He lifted his arm.

Oh-oh, I thought. He's going to punch me in the chops.

'Havoc,' he said.

Out came the arm, and—

Good Lord!

The hand was in shaking position.

'Havoc, let me congratulate you.'

And the old warhorse actually smiled.

'Congratulate him?' Goodpasture sounded as though he were strangling. 'Congratulate him?'

Bewildered, I shook with Dum-Dum, who roared, 'Why are you harassing this man, officer? And you, Bark. Why are you abusing him? My God, what's wrong with you people? This little fellow wiped out an entire spy ring! Prevented vital military secrets from leaving the country! It took me nearly two hours to find out where you'd spirited him, Bark, and believe me, I'm not too happy about it. No, sir, not too happy at all. It's obvious you have some personal grudge against him. Or perhaps you hoped to whitewash your miserable performance today by getting this clever little fellow to confess to all sorts of extra-legal charges. Well, it won't work.'

And, with a palsy smile that nearly had me fainting with surprise, old Dum-Dum put his arm around my shoulder. 'Rest assured, Havoc, I'll handle your case personally.'

'But,' said General Bark, 'but ... but ... but...'

'Oh, be quiet,' Offenbach snapped. 'I'll take care of you when I write my report on today's maneuvers. What have you been doing the last six months, Bark, reading girlie-girlie magazines all day? This little fellow single-handed—I repeat, single-handed!—showed the entire 2nd S.A.D. how to carry out a superb exercise in one-man, psychological, guerilla-type warfare! If you had a tenth of his brains, Bark, you might be getting somewhere in the service. Oh, don't shilly-shally with me, Bark! No excuses, no excuses. Of course your men tried to distort the truth and cover up for you. But I got the whole story. This little fellow here—Hammock, is it?'

'Havoc,' I said. 'John Havoc.'

'Well, Havoc, any man who can outwit an entire group of tough, trained soldiers, and decoy them by taking over their command post—that man is a comer. Yes, sir, a comer. For you, Bark,' he said, withering again, 'I have nothing but contempt. Why, your troops let themselves be demoralized by one man! They ran around like a bunch of goats! What if Havoc here had been a subversive? What about that, hey? Thank God,' he finished fervently with another clap of my shoulder, 'thank God Havoc is One of Ours.'

FitzHugh Goodpasture had one hand over his face. He was peering out from between his fingers in utter misery.

'General?' he said faintly. 'I realize, sir, that you may feel strongly about the matter,

211

but there are some civil charges for which I must hold this man.'

'What charges?' Offenbach roared.

That's when I piped up: 'He has the D.A.'s office trying to find some, General. It's a railroad job.'

'It certainly sounds like it. Well, officer, I demand this man's release. In fact,' he added darkly, 'I got that order from Washington just moments ago by phone. Orders of the Joint Chiefs. We want to interview Mr. Havoc ourselves. We might even have a spot for a man of his brilliance as a strategy planner.'

'You can't . . . !' Bark fumed.

'You mustn't . . . !' Goodpasture squeaked. He stopped. Shaking his head, he walked into the corner and stood looking at the wall.

'Well,' I said, straightening my tie, 'shall we go, General?'

'Excellent idea.' Like a couple of battlefield comrades, we strolled toward the door. 'Tell me, son. Do you know any other tricks of strategy and tactics? I'd certainly like to talk it over with you. And please call me Dum-Dum.'

'Sure, Dum-Dum. As a matter of fact, I do have a few ideas about—Judy!'

'Johnny!'

And there she was, leaping up from a bench in the outer hall. She propelled herself against my person, arms around my neck and her just-the-right-size five-foot frame pressed tightly against me.

'Johnny, I was so afraid they had put you in jail. And I've got so much to thank you for.'

She gave me a long, moist, delicious kiss. When she drew back, I gazed into her merry eyes and got a couple of flashes which said she would be thanking me in a much more tangible way, the first time we were alone. My hormones did nip-ups.

'Judy,' I said, 'may I present General D. D. Offenbach of the Joint Chiefs? Dum-Dum, this is Judy Swanson. She...'

I went blank.

Judy looked upset. 'Johnny, what on earth is the matter?'

'B. C. Chin,' I said half aloud. 'Oh my God.'

My head was spinning. While Miss Aloha Ross and Mr. Kewpie North were now in custody, along with the contents of the attaché case which had once belonged to Hopper T. Wicks, it had struck me that the Oriental Menace was still at large. And, as far as I knew, nobody knew anything about him. Certainly in all the hubbub I hadn't said anything. And I doubted that Aloha would talk, ever.

B. C. Chin had been supposed to meet Aloha to pick up the information at 6 p.m. this very evening. My watch said it was much later. But Chin would turn up again in a few days, I remembered, if she failed to show tonight. And she had failed.

'Johnny lad!' Dum-Dum said solicitously. 'Heavens, I hope it's not battle fatigue.'

'No, no, wait a minute,' I said vaguely.

My greedy little brain cells were clicking so fast I could barely keep up with them.

As far as I knew, B. C. Chin—since Aloha had told him so—still believed I was her agent. And out at the Brummel Place, I had managed to get a glom at the peanut butter, film and toothpaste info while waltzing with Kewpie and his enforcers. Suppose—I saw the dollar bills already—now suppose I typed up another report. Similar format, but fake figures.

Suppose I tricked out a black attaché case with some initials like H.T.W., and collected eighty-five thousand bucks by meeting Chin next week at the little park by the Chutes-O-Fun? I could give him a tale about having escaped the police net with the info. Aloha got caught, yes, but I escaped, and here is the material, glorious leader. Now where's the cabbage?

'It sings,' I said feverishly.

Dum-Dum blinked. 'Miss Swanson, do you know anything about his medical history?'

Green loot! And at the same time, I would be able to do my bit, finally, to obfuscate the

214

slimy enemy, and repay part of the score left
by the murders of Edson and Wicks. After a
suitable time, I could tip the authorities about
Chin and . . . huzzah!

'General?' I came back to life. 'Judy?'

'What, what?' they both cried, concerned.

'I just discovered I have enough cash in my
accounts receivable fund to take you both to
dinner.'

Judy looked miffed. 'Is that all you ever
think about, John Havoc? Money?'

'Well, not quite all,' I said, ogling her
generous assets. She giggled.

'Then let's be on our way,' said
Dum-Dum.

'Let's,' I said, linking arms.

We marched down the corridor. And while
we may not have looked much like the Spirit
of '76, for one reason and another I still
considered it a very patriotic ending.